The
Ellen Potter
Mysteries
Book One

A
Strange Encounter
at

LITTLE HUBERY

How it all begins . . .

Published by Camelot Publishing Company
4302 159th Street, Urbandale, IA 50323 U.S.A.
www.camelotpublishingco.com

PUBLISHER'S NOTE
This is a work of fiction. Names, characters, places, and
incidents, including the year Betty's Tearoom opened in York,
are the product of the author's imagination or are used
fictitiously, and any resemblance to actual persons, living or
dead, business establishments, events, or locales is entirely
coincidental.

Printed in Great Britain and in the United States of America

For my pa

A Word from the Editor

Since I began at Camelot, I've been privileged to review a wide variety of manuscripts. Few have excited me as much as *Little Hubery*.

The author's love of trains is evident in every chapter. Woven with consummate skill into the narrative are snippets of history about the railway lines and rural stations that disappeared decades ago from the British countryside.

From across the North Yorkshire Moors to a time just far enough into the past to have been forgotten by many, Phillips gathers together a group of unlikely characters and thrusts them into a set of circumstances guaranteed to bring out either the best in them or the worst in them.

Whether you are a lover of trains or not, Phillips' ability to tell a compelling tale will draw you in. This book is full of the stuff of ghost tales from days gone by, dark and spooky and creepy enough to satisfy anyone's desire for a good shiver. Its lush descriptions and quirky characters are merely the icing on this cake.

I guarantee you will want to make yourself a cup of something warm, light the fire, and curl up in your easy chair for a long, quiet evening.

Mica Rossi
U. S. Editor-in-Chief
2021

Acknowledgements

My continuing appreciation to Camelot, particularly Mica Rossi, whose support is invaluable, whose belief is incredible, and whose friendship is inimitable.

Thank you to Martin Pachacz for his kind use of the photograph in the cover illustration.

And a special thank you to the wonderfully talented Chris Bates for allowing me the use of what must be one of the most beautifully worded forewords ever.

Foreword

Nothing - but nothing - is quite as atmospheric as a railway: a village's link with the outside world, a country station where an only son set off for war, a bustling terminus where the grand and the bland go about their travels. So it follows that it throws up ghosts – of journeys past, of lovers gone, of children emigrated, of work done, and of prisoners returned.

Hustle, toil, noise, steam, smoke, joy, despair, honeymoons, deaths – all are entwined and encompassed by railways, on lines both extant and extinct...

Chris Bates 1989
Excerpted from the Foreword to
Railway Ghosts & Phantoms

The man leant against the parapet and straightened his tie. The view from bridge three-sixty-one allowed him to see for miles around, but the woodland, coastline, and untamed natural beauty of the surrounding moorland held no charm for him. Not today.

It had been another hot day and the sun was setting on the horizon, weaving braids of fiery red across the sky. The man wiped beads of perspiration from his forehead and looked at his pocket-watch. Only another ten minutes to go and then it would all be over. He thought of his fiancée and how he'd let her down. He hoped that she'd understand and that one day she'd be able to forgive him.

Five minutes now and his mouth felt parched. His hands were shaking and his vision hazy. He thought he could hear the approaching engine, the York Express, a 4-6-0 tank locomotive pulling four coaches. He heard the low whistle down the line and the faint humming of the vibrating track. He knew the engine was building up a good head of steam as it worked hard against the grade, and he heard the familiarly comforting rhythmical clunk of the side irons. He fancied he could smell the burning fuel, just whispers of smoke on the wind's breath. And then he saw her on the horizon, emerging from the tunnel like a beautiful, armoured goddess of war. A testament to power and ingenuity, her paintwork gleaming in the bright sunlight. A vision of splendour shimmering and wavering in the incandescent heat.

Trembling now, he climbed over and onto the narrow ledge, the roar becoming deafening as the train approached.

'Please God, forgive me!' he cried out in anguish. He paused for a second as he thought he heard the sweetest of voices calling out his name, and he looked around him blindly, his eyes blurred with tears. The train was but a few feet away and he knew the voice was in his head, that he would never again hear his beloved Elizabeth.

But Elizabeth was calling him… Elizabeth was there. She'd arrived at the bridge just in time to see her husband-to-be throw himself off the ledge and into the path of the oncoming train.

Little Hubery Station was opened in eighteen-ninety-two by the Malton to Redcar branch of the North Eastern Railway Company to satisfy demand for customers travelling south to the market towns of Pickering and Helmsley or north towards Middlesbrough.

A goods line had long since run along the outskirts of the hamlet known as Little Hubery, but the nearest passenger embarkation point had been Clarings Brook a little over nine miles away. Shearing's Vale, a larger station another twelve miles northwest, served goods and passengers and had lines bearing east to Whitby and the coast and west toward Darlington, as well as joining Little Hubery with stations further north.

Little Hubery lay with its back to open moorland, close enough to the coast to be able to taste the salt in the air and was totally exposed to the winds that swept off the North Sea and howled across the vast empty landscape. It was a quiet, isolated spot, the kind of place people regularly passed through on the train but rarely stopped off at. Sometimes a train would terminate there, leaving passengers to wait for the next one along to Shearing's Vale, but this was uncommon, and so Little Hubery remained a peaceful outpost.

The station itself was opened August seventeenth of that year by the then Mayor of Scarborough, Mr John Dale. It consisted of a waiting room, booking office, an admin office/storeroom with a tiny kitchen and staff convenience, the stationmaster's office, and further down the platform, the customer toilets and some small storerooms. The opposite down platform housed an additional storage room and a stone recess where commuters could shelter from the elements. Behind these were a couple of sheds, one housing coal, with a small siding and goods loop farther down the line. Beyond the sheds were a river, the stationmaster's house, and then open moorland.

It was built of local stone on two raised island platforms with a connecting bridge and was situated off a small side road. The salty sea air and the vulnerable moorland position had given the station an aged, weathered look, and the offices and waiting room remained cool during summer months and provided a cosy refuge for passengers travelling in colder weather.

Stationmaster Arthur McLaren had worked at Little Hubery since nineteen-twenty-two, inheriting the title from his late father Albert, who had retired in twenty-six. He was a proud man, and like many railway workers of his time, he was a trusted and committed employee, married to his job and entirely dependable. Arthur, a booking office clerk, two signalmen, a porter, and a part-time office lady who occasionally helped with tickets accounted for the entire staff at Little Hubery at that time.

Being isolated as it was and wearing its weathered countenance, Little Hubery Station, abandoned and locked up after closing, was the subject of many a tale from superstitious townsfolk who gathered around the inglenook in the village inn on cold winter evenings. Some of them claimed, albeit not within earshot of Arthur, that old Albert McLaren, Little Hubery's second-longest serving stationmaster, had never left and still presided over the running of the station, even in death.

Arthur, a level-headed no-nonsense kind of fellow, scoffed at ridiculous tales of hauntings in general. He'd witnessed nothing in his many years serving as stationmaster or as clerk before it, and what his eye didn't see, so his mind refused to believe in. Although he'd be the first to admit that the station did seem more than a little creepy on dark winter nights when the wind howled across the moor, bringing with it vague whisperings from disembodied voices. On nights such as these,

5

particularly before the introduction of electricity to the station, when the flickering gaslights exaggerated rather than eliminated the dark nooks and shadowy corners of the station buildings, it was easy to allow imaginations to run wild. But Hubery was his station, it was what it was, and it was hard to imagine that any station in such a lonely, isolated spot would not attract tales of a similar nature.

The stationmaster's bones creaked as he rose from his chair. He opened the door from his office and stepped outside onto the platform in good time to see the two-thirty express train to York thundering through the station.

'Hmm,' he murmured, snapping shut his pocket-watch in satisfaction. 'Not a minute before time, not a second after.'

He looked up at the clouds that hung ominously over the station. It had been threatening rain all day, and the wind had been getting up for the last couple of hours.

'We're in for a belter of a storm,' he said to himself, trying not to give in to the feelings of despondency that arose from time to time when working in an isolated moorland spot. He thought of the mountain of paperwork he had to get through that afternoon and how a good fire, a cup of tea, and Alistair Cook on the wireless would improve his mood.

The stationmaster nodded to a couple of passengers who had just emerged from the booking office, presumably waiting for the next train in, the two-forty-five to Redcar.

Around him the moorland was eerily quiet, only a distant rumble of thunder breaking the peaceful repose. From somewhere far off came the lonely cry of a hawk out on the moor, and the first few drops of rain caught on the wind and settled on his nose and eyelashes. Another peal of thunder, closer this time, and the stationmaster couldn't suppress a shudder.

The couple walked arm-in-arm along to the other end of the platform and the bridge. The young man said something, and the girl giggled.

'I really don't like the look of those clouds,' thought the stationmaster as he opened the waiting room door. After checking on Percy, his clerk, he made for his office and switched on his wireless, trying hard to combat the feelings of unease that were gaining momentum as the day went on. As though reading his thoughts, the presenter greeted Arthur with a newsflash and severe weather warnings of freak clusters of storms moving inland along the east coast. Low pressure here, coupled with unusually high winds from over there... The stationmaster groaned. Freak storms, unseasonable weather patterns. It was more like a doomsday prediction.

'Pull yourself together, old boy,' he chided. 'You've a station to run.' But he found himself looking at the clock and thinking of home, nonetheless.

Chapter Three

Professor Victor Rose tried to stifle a yawn. He'd had a long journey starting at London King's Cross, and he still had to make a couple of changes and travel another ninety-odd miles before he was home. He had journeyed to London to pick up a rare book he'd bought from an antiquarian bookseller in Paddington. Prior to this, he had visited his friend, Professor Sidney Miles, Dean of Faculty at King's College Cambridge, in whose company he had enjoyed first class hospitality and a fine single malt, not to mention intellectual discourse with his former colleague and his students.

Professor Rose enjoyed his bi-annual visits to his beloved Cambridge, but they really tired him out and he was looking forward to seeing hearth and home again. He lived in a cosy cottage by the sea in Saltburn with his dog Scout and his house-keeper Mrs Carr, and apart from the aforementioned, he rarely saw another soul. His was a quiet, peaceful, and quite unremarkable life, and he liked it that way. A self-confirmed bachelor, he had dedicated his life to the pursuit of learning. His small library, his coastal walks, and Mrs Carr's fine cooking were all he needed to live a full and contented life.

His train arrived at Doncaster, where a few got off and even fewer got on. A family of four with two very excited boys joined him in his carriage and seemed bound for their holidays in Edinburgh. Their father was teasing them about joining a haggis hunt when they got to Scotland, and the little boys' eyes shone with anticipation. The professor couldn't suppress a smile as one of the boys asked if the hunt would be on horseback, and the boys' mother clicked her tongue in feigned annoyance at her husband's teasing. They soon settled in and gave up their tickets to the inspector, and Victor relaxed back into his seat and closed his eyes for a moment.

'Mustn't sleep,' he mumbled to himself, fearing he would lose his connection. He would soon be in York, where he planned to have a nice cup of tea and a pastry before catching the train to Malton.

Chapter Four

In the next carriage, Sir Gregory Barnes, knighted for services to the bar and recently retired, grumbled and muttered under his breath. He hated train journeys. All the fuss and bother, the dirty, overcrowded stations, and as for the trains themselves! Travelling shoulder to shoulder across the length and breadth of the countryside with people from all walks of life, it really was a tiresome mode of transport and one quite unsuitable for a gentleman of his standing.

Taking the Flying Scotsman to York from London, where he and his wife had spent a few days with their son, was one thing. From thereon in they were consigned to travelling along branch lines whose trains were quite provincial and whose frequent changes were nothing short of criminal. York to Malton and then change at Malton for the Redcar train, disembark at Shearing's Vale where his man was to pick him up and drive him to Beechings, his country pile, hopefully in good time for dinner.

His wife, Lady Agnes, was a placid, good-natured woman who, far from hating train journeys, secretly enjoyed them and looked forward to travelling by Flying Scotsman with all the relish of a schoolboy on his first trip aboard a locomotive. When it came to travelling on the branch lines, however, she was in full agreement with her husband, as the trains were often late and run-down, with hard and uncomfortable horse-hair seating and dirty windows. The train to Shearing's Vale was particularly unpleasant, a two coach, non-corridor, snorting beast of a train, quite often crowded and always cold and poorly maintained. Unfortunately, it was either this or a direct train from York to Redcar and having to return at Redcar on the same grotty little train all the way back to Shearing's Vale. She was hoping however, as they would be returning quite late to the Vale, that the train would be less packed.

She looked across at her husband and smiled to herself. He was a dreadful snob, and she often wondered what people thought of him. He was a proud man and had been one of the country's top barristers. But he had been slowing down recently and his hands were gnarled and crippled by arthritis. His temper hadn't been curbed any, though.

Pompous old fool, she thought, smiling fondly. Sir Gregory looked up from his newspaper and wondered what was amusing his wife so.

Chapter Five

Miss Ellen Potter had been offered a position as head of English and literature studies at a boarding school for girls in Northumberland and was taking the journey to begin her new post.

Instead of taking the train direct from York where she lived with her sister, she had taken the train to Malton and would change there for Redcar, where she would stay with an elderly relative who'd not been too well recently. It would mean her starting with her new school a little late into the new term, but all was set, and the school was quite happy with the arrangement.

She didn't mind the detour. She thought a trip across the wild Yorkshire moorland would be exciting. Maybe she would see the gloomy, austere form of Wuthering Heights from her carriage window, or the burnt-out shell of the Rochester house up on the hill. Maybe she'd meet her Heathcliff on the train, a dark and brooding stranger who would catch her eye and whisk her off to a life as lady of the manor. In her mid-twenties, Ellen's head was still as full of romantic notions as it had been at eighteen, although for a lady nearing spinster age, and one in her position as department head at the school, she really should have known better.

She was lucky to have been offered such a good position, but the school had been in dire need of a replacement teacher and that, along with her exemplary reference from her last employer and the fact that her Aunt Iris, whom she was on her way to see, had been headmistress there, had stood her in good stead with the school. She knew her sister and her aunt had conspired to get her out of York as quickly as possible, and understandably. For reasons known only to herself, she blushed a deep shade of crimson, quickly burying her head in her bag under the pretence of fishing for her compact so that no-one could witness her indignity.

It had been a truly messy affair but not one entirely of her own making. She thought of George and brushed away a tear before composing herself and powdering her nose, quickly snapping shut her mirror after receiving a look of disdain from an elderly lady, who was passing.

She longed for a cigarette but thought momentarily of her Aunt Iris, who disapproved of ladies smoking in public. Although Ellen was single-minded, learned, and strong-willed, she always felt extremely uncomfortable under the glare of older ladies and was, in truth, far more at ease in the company of children. She looked forward to the safe and comfortable confines of the school where she might begin writing her long-planned novel. She knew she would have a good life there, although she had not given up entirely on meeting her Mr Darcy.

She thought she might treat herself to a new book from Smiths, the newsagent. A Bronte classic perhaps, or maybe even the new Agatha Christie novel if she could get hold of it. Who better than the mistress of suspense when you're looking through a train carriage window at a desolate, storm-tossed moor?

Through the refreshment room window, the platform was lit by flashes of lightning. Ellen was much affected by atmospherics, and as she looked out at the gathering clouds, a sudden shiver of excitement ran up and down her spine. She was looking forward to starting her new life at the school, but she had a growing feeling of unease that she couldn't quite fathom. Nerves, perhaps, at the thought of her new position.

'Snap out of it, Ellen,' she chided.

As she stood sharply and turned to leave, she felt the room shifting around her, a strange feeling, not at all like light-headedness, but it caused her to grab the chairback nonetheless for fear of falling. Dark images filled Ellen's mind, more flashes than thoughts, memories best left buried but powerful enough to cause her to grimace, to crease her brow, so that anyone witnessing it from outside on the platform would be left to wonder at what unpleasant notions could darken so lovely a face.

Chapter Six

Lance Corporal Robert Newton, of the newly amalgamated 4th/7th Royal Dragoon Guards, pulled the collar of his overcoat tight around his neck against the biting wind that seemed to whip up from nowhere. He lit a cigarette, shielding the flame from the elements, and wandered up and down the empty platform. He had never seen Malton so quiet. Harrogate in contrast had been a hive of activity, and he was secretly glad to be away from the crowds. Peace and quiet was just what he needed now, time to think.

He'd been in India for the past six months and was now to be stationed at Catterick Camp. He was currently on leave and had been visiting his mother in Harrogate before going to meet his wife and daughter in Redcar. He sat down on the bench and ran his hand across his face. He wasn't at all looking forward to the inquiry he would face when his leave was over. He thought of the incident that had prompted it and of its potential consequences. Talk about wrong place, wrong time! Damn him, that fellow had deserved everything he got, no-one could deny that. Robert hadn't been involved directly but he hadn't exactly been forthcoming either, as a keeper of the peace or as a witness.

He wrung his hands and a shadow fell across his troubled face when he thought of what had passed and what was to follow as a consequence. He knew he was early and had a long wait for his train, but everything seemed drawn out and tiresome to him since that day three weeks ago. Truth was, nobody knew he'd witnessed the event. He realised people could place him close to the scene, but nobody could prove he'd actually watched the action unfold from where he was positioned. Should he lie to save himself and his colleagues and friends, or tell the truth and face the consequences?

A sudden streak of lightning lit up the platform like a flare, and Lance Corporal Robert Newton stubbed out his cigarette underfoot and buried his head deeper into his overcoat.

On the opposite platform, from the window of a shadowy waiting room, a silent figure watched.

Chapter Seven

Percy shovelled the remaining pieces of coal onto the waiting room fire before refilling the scuttle from a small coal store behind the station buildings, used for the station fires and the stove in the signal box. They'd be turning the platform lights on soon, as well as those inside the station. It was getting dark early now and the bloody storm clouds didn't help any. He could have sworn he heard thunder a couple of minutes ago.

He couldn't shake off the unsettled feeling he'd had all day. He didn't like storms at the best of times, not since he was about seven and he'd seen his friend struck by lightning as they played on the moor. This one was set to be a right humdinger. There'd be trouble on the line for certain if the storm broke, especially with the wind getting up. Power cuts too, no doubt.

He could hear the wireless from Arthur's office, and he knew the BBC had just announced a severe weather warning for all coastal stations. Arthur was much affected by the weather, and he was certainly in a strange mood today.

'I'll take him a cup of tea in a minute or two,' Percy thought. 'That ought to cheer him up a bit.'

He found himself feeling thankful for the gas stove at the station, not to mention the old gas lamps, should the power be cut.

'I'd hate to be at the mercy of electricity alone,' he thought, and sighed.

A sudden pelt of rain on the windows made him look up, and the young couple who'd just left the waiting room came running in breathless and laughing, equally surprised by the suddenness of the downpour.

'We're in for one tonight,' the young man commented to Percy. 'Better batten down the hatches. That wind's getting up something fierce. I hope there are no cancellations to trains. We've a distance to go yet.'

'Well, we've heard nothing so far, sir,' Percy replied. 'But I'll certainly keep you posted if we do.'

Professor Rose was sure he'd seen the gentleman who'd just entered the refreshment room somewhere before.

'Oh dear,' said the woman at the gentleman's elbow, 'it's rather full, isn't it?'

The professor stood and motioned the couple over.

'You're more than welcome to join me at my table,' he offered with a smile. 'I'm afraid you'll never find a quiet time to visit York Station.'

'Awful journey home,' Sir Gregory said, after introducing himself and his wife. 'And now the weather's turned.'

'And set to get worse I'm afraid,' said Professor Rose, smiling at Lady Agnes. 'Have you far to go?'

The conversation was interrupted by two young lads who tore into the refreshment room, chased each other around the tables, and then fled when an angry-looking man came out from behind the counter.

'Young hooligans. Should be publicly flogged,' bellowed Sir Gregory, and one or two turned in their seats to look at him. Lady Agnes smiled sheepishly at the professor, whose newly-arrived pastry had suddenly demanded his utmost attention.

'Of course,' said the professor, smiling as they settled down into their carriage on the train. 'I thought I recognised you. You were the judge in that kidnapping case, with the little boy. Dreadful business that. The fellow hanged, I believe?'

'He did,' said Sir Gregory. 'But hanging was too good for him after what he did to that poor boy. Given the choice, I'd have had him on the rack. A prolonged and painful death is all a scoundrel like that deserves.'

The professor winced and Lady Agnes smiled apologetically.

'Come now, Gregory. Justice has been served and the man has paid the ultimate price for his crime. Let God be his judge now.'

'Hmm!' grumbled Sir Gregory. 'And may he be condemned to burn in hellfire forevermore! Now, let that be an end to it. Where's my newspaper?'

Professor Rose smiled as Lady Agnes raised her eyes to heaven in exasperation. Soon enough, the compartment was quiet as the journey progressed and the two gentlemen settled down to their papers, only the occasional moan from Sir Gregory about the hard, unyielding seats or his nagging arthritis breaking the silence as they steamed across the darkening, windswept moor.

Ellen noticed the young soldier sitting on the platform at Malton and thought him rather handsome. She walked past him to the bench further down and took out her new Agatha Christie novel, *Murder in Mesopotamia*. He glanced briefly, appreciating the female form, but it was clear his mind was elsewhere. She thought about going to the waiting room as it was starting to rain, but the train was due soon and the waiting room was down the far end of the platform, so she decided to stay put.

She thought how unhurried the station was for the time of day. Apart from herself and the soldier, it seemed only a handful or so, including the two elderly gentlemen and the rather well-dressed lady, were waiting for the train to Redcar. She didn't mind that at all. It meant she could read in peace and daydream to her heart's content. In fact, she hoped to have a compartment to herself.

Soon the two coach non-corridor train pulled alongside the platform, and its passengers climbed aboard eagerly, happy to continue their respective journeys out of the biting wind. Ellen looked through the window of one compartment and was startled by the face that stared back at her. It was a face she knew, whose dark, hate-filled eyes glared at her with pure malice. Her heart began to pound, and she felt a trickle of perspiration run down her back. For what seemed like an age, she was unable to pull away.

'But it couldn't be her,' she told herself.

A sheet of newspaper, caught in the wind, attached itself to the carriage window, hiding the other's face from view. The headline emblazoned across the page made Ellen's blood run cold.

PROMINENT SCHOOLMASTER'S WIFE CRITICAL FOLLOWING ATTEMPT ON LIFE

'It couldn't be. It's impossible.'

She walked quickly down to the next coach and saw the three distinguished elders and the soldier climbing into the second and third compartments. She hastily jumped into the first, her heart beating wildly, fear shrouding her like a widow's cape.

'Impossible,' she repeated, closing her eyes and breathing deeply, trying to regain composure. She was joined seconds before departure by an older lady who smiled at her sweetly before settling down with her book. Ellen smiled back, suddenly glad of the company.

As the train pulled out of the station, she could see two or three people milling about on the platform. An angry-looking man was bending the ear of a poor porter, and a beautiful young girl caught her eye before quickly looking away. Ellen thought how sad and lost the girl had looked and found herself wondering about her fellow travellers and where their journeys would lead them.

Soon her attention was drawn to the craggy moorland beyond the rain-lashed window. The occasional lonely dwelling, cosy and lamp-lit, looked to Ellen like a beacon on a storm-tossed sea and made her feel alone and displaced. The wind howled across the open moor, buffeting the train. When the lightning flashed, bathing the wilderness beyond in an eerie glow, she imagined she could see all manner of unearthly creatures lurking in the bushes and waiting in the shadows to engulf them in the event of the train stopping and their being stranded out there on the wild moor.

She picked up her book and wished she had bought something a little more light-hearted.

'Soon be home, dear.' The old lady smiled at her kindly, sensing her growing unease. Ellen thought of her aunt's fire-lit parlour and a good hot supper and settled back into her seat and rested her eyes.

Alone in his compartment, Robert was feeling increasingly agitated. He lit another cigarette and noticed the slight trembling of his hand. It wasn't the storm that bothered him, nor was he unduly concerned about the enquiry to come. He had, in fact, decided that he would feign ignorance of any knowledge of the incident. He was only being called as a potential witness, after all. It was the only option if he was to carry on with his military career. His own survival and that of his family depended on it.

Given the option of turning back time, he would certainly have intervened. Stopped his comrades short of taking the man's life, however much he deplored him for what he was and the abominations he had committed. But there was nothing he could do now. The man was dead! Ruining the lives and careers of three good men wouldn't bring him back. His decision was made.

Even with the weight of the decision off his shoulders, Robert still felt uneasy. It was a creepy sensation, almost like a feeling of impending doom. His stomach was tense and knotted, and his throat was dry. He looked out at the moor just as a flash of lightning illuminated the backdrop. Through the sparkle of raindrops on the grimy window, he saw this particular part of the moorland was thick with shrub, and he imagined, as he stared into the wilderness, a thousand pairs of accusing eyes watching him from deep within the shadowy leaves and prickly hedgerows. His unease deepened as a sudden, ominous sensation washed over him.

Turning away from the scene, he rested his head against the wall and closed his eyes until the feeling subsided.

Chapter Nine

The station at Little Hubery had been quiet all afternoon since the departure of the young couple on the two-forty-five to Redcar. 'Fledglings,' Percy thought and smiled. He had visions of his own wife and felt a pain akin to mourning. His marriage was in trouble, he could not deny it. He loved Dorothy more than life itself, but his uncontrollable fits of jealousy were ruining everything. Since she'd taken up painting classes at the church hall, his imagination had run riot and with no evidence or provocation at all. What the hell was wrong with him? Why couldn't he just enjoy being loved?

He heard Arthur through the door singing along to Guy Lombardo's 'You're Driving Me Crazy.'

'You've got that about right, my friend,' he thought grimly. Maybe Arthur had the right idea, living the uncomplicated bachelor life.

All at once, he was overcome by a feeling of someone having walked over his grave. The lightning flashed in the distance, followed by the roar of thunder, and the station lights flickered once, then flickered twice more in succession, before turning out completely. The rain, carried by gale force winds, beat against the windows with gusto. The waiting room grew considerably darker, and even though the fire burned well enough in the grate, colder too it seemed! Percy shivered.

'This bloody station is creepy enough at the best of times without this awful storm,' he thought, rubbing his arms to keep warm.

'Percy,' called out Arthur from his office. 'It seems the lights have gone out.'

As Percy walked through to the back office, he was aware that he could hear Arthur's wireless.

'Odd,' said Arthur as though reading his mind. 'The radio's still on.'

'Can't be the bulb,' said Percy, reaching up and tapping it with his fingernails. 'They're out in the waiting room, too.'

'Perhaps the storm has in some way affected the lighting circuit, Percy. You should turn on the gas lamps,' Arthur replied.

Percy lit a taper and was about to turn on the gas when all of a sudden he felt certain he was being watched and that whoever it was, was right behind him. He'd not heard the waiting room door go, and Arthur was still in his office. He turned slowly and gasped when he saw the man standing there. He was tall, much taller than Percy who was by no means a small man, but painfully thin. His hair, his skin, even his suit, which was bone-dry although he carried no coat or umbrella, were waxy and grey. His eyes, which were also a faded grey, were soulless and empty. Percy couldn't suppress a shudder when the man suddenly smiled at him, a grim, sinister smile that never quite reached his eyes.

'Single, first to Redcar, please.' The man's voice was monotonous and low, and Percy could barely make out his words over the sudden clap of thunder that seemed so much closer than the last.

But where had he come from? Percy was sure he hadn't entered by the platform. The only other way was through the booking office, and he'd been in there the whole time.

'The Redcar train will terminate here, sir, due to signalling problems at Clarings Brook. I'm not sure when the next through train will be on account of the weather.

The man's smile never waned and seemed to Percy as if it were painted on.

'Never mind,' he said. 'I'm quite happy waiting here.'

Another streak of lightning and his face was bathed in an eerie glow, highlighting the waxen pallor of his skin, the shadows accentuating the sunken hollows of his eyes.

'Pull yourself together Percy,' the clerk thought, turning his head away. 'The poor man's obviously ill.'

Percy waited until the man had seated himself beside the fire, noticing how even the glow of the flames failed to add warmth to his dead skin. He wondered as to how a man could walk across a wooden floor and sit on a creaky wooden chair barely making a sound. Everything about him was odd. As the stranger pulled out a newspaper from his briefcase and began to read, the sinister smile that had so unnerved Percy on first meeting him, remained. He was still staring at the man when Arthur walked through from his office.

'Does the gentleman know that the next train terminates here, Percy?'

Percy jumped. He hadn't heard Arthur come in.

'Percy?'

'Erm, yes. Yes, I told him. He said he's happy to wait.'

Arthur sighed and approached the passenger.

'Good afternoon, sir,' said Arthur. 'I'm sorry for your wait. It's just a minor signalling problem, and we hope to have it fixed soon.'

The man looked up from his paper at the stationmaster. 'No problem at all. I'm in no hurry and quite content sitting here.'

The shrill ringing of the telephone had Arthur hurrying back to his office.

He knew he'd never be able to keep her in the style she'd been accustomed to. The Mayor's daughter, how could he? Him, a simple bank clerk. What did he have to offer a lady like that, really? Everyone was surprised when they became a couple and even more so when she accepted his proposal. But he knew she genuinely loved him as he did her, with all his heart.

He'd heard a rumour that Mr Sykes, the assistant bank manager, was to retire, and if he did, that meant that Norman would be next in line for *that* job, leaving a supervisory position vacant. Surely now it was *his* turn to move up the ranks? God knows he'd been there long enough. How proud of him Betty would be then, and it meant more money. He could buy her that ring she wanted from the jewellers in the high street.

He was doing well at the bank. No-one could deny that. Why only that morning he'd taken in four new accounts. Lucrative ones, too. Fat landlords looking for somewhere to deposit their tenants' weekly payments. Hundreds of pounds they had in their accounts. He'd looked on enviously as they made their deposits, thinking how a few shillings of that a week into his own account would make a world of difference. Just a shilling or two, always from different accounts.

Nobody would miss it… would they?

Chapter Ten

Little Hubery Station stood bleached by lightning, its rough stonework standing out against the darkening backdrop of the moor. Through the tall windows, the flickering, amber glow of the fire made the station seem cosy and welcoming to the disheartened passengers who left the terminated Redcar train and crossed the bridge. A man in a military coat, a young woman, two elderly gents and a well-dressed lady of advancing years were the only passengers left on the train when it was forced to terminate at Little Hubery. Although clearly upset at having their journey disrupted, only one of the older gentlemen made a fuss.

The train standing at the platform redirected to the siding in preparation for its return to Malton. The passengers joined the other traveller already in the waiting room, but he seemed not to notice their arrival, never once looking up from his newspaper as they noisily crowded around the fire.

'It appears we may be here for some time,' said the professor. 'Have you been here long, sir?' he asked the man already seated.

'Hardly any time at all,' the man replied.

'I've lit the lamps on the platform, Arthur. Would you like me to stay on? Looks like you'll be here for quite a while.' Percy looked in on the stationmaster when the ticket office closed. He would often walk home from the station to his cottage on the other side of Little Hubery, unless the weather turned really cold. Then he would catch a lift home with Wilfred, the station porter, but the urgent call his boss had received was to report a tree on the line further up, so it looked as though Arthur would have a fair bit to deal with yet. Not least the six passengers in the waiting room, some of whom seemed to be growing agitated and nervous, the heightening storm undoubtedly playing its part.

'I'll be fine, Percy,' said Arthur, looking up from his paperwork. 'I'll put a call through to Clarings Brook and then I'll speak to the passengers. How are they?' He nodded towards the waiting room where the displaced passengers were gathered.

'I didn't go in, but I could hear them grumbling from the ticket office,' Percy replied. 'They seem a bit restless, and there's one gentleman kicking up a stink, but they're mostly fine. Arthur...' Percy paused hesitantly. 'Did you notice anything odd about that man who arrived before the others came off the train?'

'Not at all,' said Arthur, throwing down his pen. 'Why do you ask?'

Percy shrugged his shoulders.

'Ah, nothing much.' He grinned. 'Just seemed a bit, well, queer is all. Anyway, I'll be off then if there's nothing else I can do.'

'No more trains for the foreseeable future folks,' said Arthur, coming in from his office. 'I'm really sorry.'

A collective moan could be heard from the passengers in the waiting room. It hung in the air like a mist.

'What's the meaning of this?' stormed one of the elderly gentlemen. 'My man is waiting with the car at Shearing's Vale.'

'I'm sorry Mr…?'

'The name is Barnes, *Sir* Gregory Barnes,' he huffed. 'I demand to know—'

'If you would all please sit down. On top of signalling failure, there's now a fallen tree on the line at Shearing's Vale. I'm afraid no-one's going anywhere from this station for a while.'

'But you don't understand, sir. My need to travel is somewhat urgent. My elderly Aunt is unwell and...' The younger lady who had been sat in a shadowy corner, previously unseen by the stationmaster, stepped forward. She clutched tightly at her suitcase and seemed concerned.

'I'm sorry, Miss…?' said Arthur.

'Potter. Ellen Potter.'

'Miss Potter. The nearest village is Little Hubery. The bus goes from there. But that's over a mile and half away across moorland and in this weather, I—'

'Oh, dear,' said Ellen pointedly. 'And you have no idea when the next train will be?'

'You mean to tell me we're stranded?' Sir Gregory interrupted, his face red with exasperation. 'But surely man, there's some mode of transport to get us to Shearing's Vale, or perhaps my man could pick me up from here?'

'I'm afraid I have no car, sir, and my porter, who has a motorcycle, has just left. Anyhow, as I was saying to the young lady, you'll find no trackless leaving Hubery tonight. And it would seem, according to the stationmaster at Clarings Brook, that there's no traffic getting through from Shearing's anyway, as the road up there is flooding. Otherwise, your gentleman *could* pick you up from here. I can call the station there and have word sent to him if you like, but it may be prudent for you to send him home…'

Ellen sighed resignedly and returned to her seat. As though giving credence to the stationmaster's

42

statement, the wind suddenly howled and drove the rain hard against the windows. A flash of lightning followed, and a loud crack of thunder was heard overhead.

'But that's absurd—' Barnes' words were cut off, and Lady Agnes gave a little shriek and clutched her husband's arm.

'You're perfectly safe in here.' Arthur smiled kindly at the older woman, who returned his infectious smile before wrinkling up her nose.

'Oh, dear, that smell,' she said. 'I feel quite lightheaded.'

'I'm afraid I can't smell anything, madam. Perhaps it's the gas lamps,' said the stationmaster, humouring the old lady. 'The mains power supply is unreliable at the best of times in a remote spot like this.'

Arthur found himself once more under the onslaught of the judge's complaints.

'...circumstances beyond my control, sir... not within my power to do so... doing all I can to rectify...'

The judge would hardly let the poor man finish and the other passengers, Lady Agnes included, marvelled at his patience.

'I suggest we let the man speak.'

The soldier stepped forward. Sir Gregory turned to him angrily, ready to answer back, but something in the soldier's manner made him think again.

'Thank you,' the stationmaster continued. 'I tried to phone the village myself, sir. There's an inn there where you might be more comfortable, but I can't get through. I am unable to leave my post, but perhaps a couple of the gentlemen might find it prudent to walk into town? You, sir,' he said to the man seated in the chimneybreast. 'Are you local? You might go with them. Perhaps you could send someone back with a car?'

The man looked up from his paper. The light was weak and cast dark shadows in the corners of the room, and just how he could see to read in that shadowy nook was anyone's guess. A strange smile played about his lips momentarily, and when he turned, his eyes shone in the glow of the fire. It seemed to anyone watching as though he was enjoying the commotion.

'I'm not local, no sir,' he replied. 'But I know well the unpredictability and the wildness of the moor, and I think I'd rather stay here, if no-one minds.'

'Really!' said Sir Gregory incredulously. 'What kind of fellow are you?' The man merely smiled

44

again and carried on reading. Sir Gregory was furious.

'I'll go!' said the professor. 'Perhaps...' he said, nodding to the soldier, 'this young man will come with me?'

'You can't go, Professor Rose,' protested Lady Agnes. She looked at the stationmaster pleadingly. 'Is there no-one else at the station, sir?'

The soldier came forward. 'I'll go alone,' he said. 'I'll send back a car.' Buttoning up his overcoat, he made for the door and grabbed the proffered torch from the stationmaster's hand.

'Be careful, sir, please!' Arthur called out over the howling wind. 'The moor is dangerous. Please don't stray from the path—'

The door slammed and his sentence was cut off.

'I hope he will be safe,' said Lady Agnes anxiously.

'I'm sure he will,' said Sir Gregory. 'Fellow had a local accent. I'm sure he's no stranger to the moor.'

The stationmaster looked at him coldly. 'We may have to stay here for the next few hours, until the storm dies down or the roads are cleared. Wireless says we're in for an almighty storm, but we've plenty of coal for the fire, and I've tea and Horlicks in my office, if you're not afraid to drink from mugs.'

'Dear God,' said Sir Gregory, sitting back down and rubbing his arthritic knees.

'I'll fetch some more coal and get a good blaze going. I suggest you try making yourselves comfortable, at least for now.'

Ellen stood up. 'I'll help you with the tea,' she said. The stationmaster thanked her, and the two left the waiting room to its subdued silence.

Chapter Eleven

Robert stepped out onto the platform, the biting wind stinging the exposed flesh of his face and lashing him with rain. Lightning illuminated the scene, and he was certain he saw a fleeting shadow at the end of the platform. Maybe there was someone else at the station after all.

'Hello!' he called out, but the wind must have carried his voice because the figure disappeared down towards the track.

Am I seeing things? Robert thought. It was very dark out there, the wind having blown out several of the gas lanterns.

'Hello!' Robert turned on the torch the stationmaster had given him, but the light was dim, scarcely reaching the platform's edge. He felt certain the man had heard him before because he had turned, and the soldier had seen his pale face, moonlit by a brief break in the clouds. Robert flashed the torch and waved, and the figure seemed to freeze for a moment.

'Hello there, sir. Can you help us?' Robert called out again, but the figure turned and ran down onto the tracks and out of sight.

When Robert stepped out of the shelter of the station buildings and onto the quiet side road, he felt the full force of the storm.

'Arrgh!' he cried out, shielding his face as he staggered backwards. Lightning flashed overhead, and then came a roar of thunder. Again the landscape lit up before him. He could see the road ahead, the only road into town across open moorland. If he accidentally wandered from the path, he could easily be lost on the moor. As a soldier, he was well used to trekking across rough terrain, but the moor was fully exposed to the elements, and the ground would be sodden and hard to tackle. What if he came across an area of marshland? They were so close to the sea, he could easily walk into a bog. No-one would hear his cries on a stormy night like this. No-one would be there to help him.

Tentatively, he made his way toward the open moor. Overhead the moon was now totally obscured by the clouds that rolled like angry waves on a storm-tossed sea. To the left-hand side of the road was fencing leading to the station. This would help him at least part of the way. While ever he felt the rough wood at his shoulder, he knew he was sticking to the path, but he tripped and fell heavily on the uneven surface of the verge, the torch falling from his open hand onto the road and rolling away from him before the light went out completely. He cursed. He knew he shouldn't go on. Only a fool would attempt to do so in such conditions.

He was already soaked through, and he could feel the rain running down the back of his collar and penetrating the soft leather of his boots. His skin felt tight against the vicious wind, and he could barely see ahead of him. What dangers did he face from vehicles out on an open road on a night like this?

Alas, he knew he had to go on. Once more he cursed his stupidity in offering to go and wished more than anything he hadn't left the warmth of the waiting room hearth.

Chapter Twelve

Three people regarded each another in morose silence. The waiting room was full of ethereal shapes cast by the dimly lit gaslights, but a good fire blazed in the grate and the wretched shadows, bathed in its amber light, danced maniacally across the walls and ceiling. A clock ticked sonorously above the mantelpiece, but even that was silenced by the deafening roar of the wind that sped along the hollow, hitting the exposed station building with full force and rattling the ill-fitting windows in their frames.

'I hope that young man will be safe out there on the moor,' began Lady Agnes.

'Fellow's trained for that kind of thing,' replied her husband gruffly. 'So long as he returns or sends a car soon, we should be just fine. I should hate to miss a good dinner.'

The professor gave the man a good hard stare, and from his place by the fire, the stranger grinned and shook his head.

'Are you going far, Mr...?' The professor turned to look at the man who had, for the most part, remained silent.

'Travers,' said the man, smiling. 'And it would appear not.'

Lady Agnes looked over and was about to introduce herself and her husband when Travers dropped his head, signifying that he had no wish for further conversation. The booking office door opened, and the stationmaster and younger woman returned, armed with mugs of hot tea and biscuits.

'Make way for the cup that cheers.' The stationmaster smiled, and despite grumblings from the judge about the state of the mugs, they were all grateful for the drinks. Travers, being closest, got up a decent blaze. Then Arthur went next door and brought in the wireless. The professor looked up in surprise.

'Only the lighting is affected, it seems,' said Arthur. 'Strange, isn't it?'

'Very odd indeed,' remarked the professor. 'Still, we should be grateful for small mercies.' So, amid the Al Bowlly and Artie Shaw sets, they listened out for the news and weather reports.

'I couldn't help but overhearing, dear, you saying that your aunt was unwell,' said Lady Agnes, turning to the handsome young woman who was sipping her tea and staring somewhat distractedly into the flames. 'I hope you're able to join her soon.'

'Yes, I fear for her well-being,' replied Ellen worriedly. 'Hers is not a serious illness, but my aunt is frail, and a storm like this can hardly be conducive to calming the nerves.'

'Will you be staying with her long?'

'Not for very long. I have a new situation as head of department at St. Barnabas School for Young Ladies in Northumberland. The term has already begun but I….'

'Excellent,' began the professor. 'One should not underestimate the importance of a good—'

Suddenly the lights in the waiting room dimmed. The flames from the gas lamps flickered and spluttered as though a draught had crept in from somewhere and was threatening to blow them clean out. Even the light from the fire was subdued. The flames seemed to cower behind the larger chunks of coal, and the clock above the mantle became unnervingly loud.

The howling of the wind out on the moor now sounded more like the cries of animals in distress, an eerie, wailing sound. The ladies looked at each other, wide-eyed and nervous. Even the men huddled a little closer to the hearth.

'Don't worry folks.' The stationmaster smiled reassuringly at Ellen and Lady Agnes. 'The station has withstood more severe weather than this and stands to tell the tale. Pity the poor signalmen isolated in their boxes or the gangers out trying to clear the line. There's always folks worse off than yourselves.'

Lady Agnes smiled back at the man with his kind, twinkling eyes and his infectious optimism and was about to agree when a strange, high-pitched whistling sound silenced all. The wireless, in the middle of playing Cab Calloway, suddenly cut off and all was silent. For a moment or two only static could be heard, and then it seemed as though someone was retuning the instrument. There were snatches of what sounded like foreign radio stations before the announcement of an urgent broadcast. All turned expectantly towards the receiver, but the voice that emanated from it wasn't that of the broadcaster. It was slow, deep and dragged out as if being wound down to such an extent, the words were hard to decipher. All the passengers could make out was '...all judgements will be passed...' and '...before this night ends.'

'Oh dear!' said Lady Agnes, and Ellen remembered the face on the train and shuddered.

'What's the meaning of this, sir?' said the barrister, turning to face the stationmaster. 'Is this meant to be some kind of joke? Because if it is I—'

From a dark corner behind Ellen, there came a low chuckle, evil and sinister. She screamed and jumped up, moving close to Lady Agnes, who put a maternal arm around her shoulder.

'Who's there?' bellowed Sir Gregory. 'Come out, man, and make yourself known.'

Arthur rushed to the back of the waiting room, but there was no-one there. He turned to face the others in bewilderment. All at once, the wind got up and the flames raced up the chimney to meet it. An overhead clap of thunder was so loud that it had the ladies wincing. The stationmaster stood dumbstruck in the far corner, and the wireless returned to 'Minnie the Moocher' as if nothing had happened.

A brief flash of lightning illuminated the scene, highlighting the professor's strange expression. He was staring into the shadows of the chimneybreast at Travers who stared back, his eyes shining with excitement and a strange, ominous smile about his lips.

Chapter Thirteen

Robert's eyes had become accustomed to the dark, but his vision was still impeded by the wind and rain which seemed much worse out here on the exposed moor. He had left the security of the fence behind a good way back, and only the firmness of the road underfoot guided him along his way. He needed to be careful not to go wandering into the middle of the road and into the path of any approaching vehicles, but the further into his journey he got, the less likely it seemed that anyone would be out there on the moor in this foul weather.

Why was he here anyway? Why was he wandering the stricken moor alone on a night like this? He didn't mind being holed up in the station for a couple of hours. Certainly his wife would worry a little if he was late, but he was sure the stationmaster would allow him to call her. Anyway, that didn't warrant him risking life and limb so the pompous old bastard back at the station could be home in time for dinner.

He turned and tried to gauge the distance between himself and the station. He seemed to have been out there for ages, but in truth he couldn't have come more than a quarter of a mile.

He was suddenly aware of another presence, and with all the sharpened senses and awareness of a soldier who had seen action, he knew that he was being watched. The moorland lit up again briefly, and he scanned the landscape, looking for signs of a predator. The land lay flat and treeless around him. There was nowhere to hide. All the same, he somehow knew he was being hunted, that unseen eyes watched him from out on the desolate moor. He felt exposed and vulnerable and turned this way and that, not knowing whether to turn back or move on, unsure in which direction the danger lurked but knowing that someone or something lay in wait for him in the darkness.

The wind screamed like a banshee, and he felt disorientated, lost for a moment. The lightning flashed, and he saw shadows moving out there on the wild, inhospitable moorland. Then all at once, the wind died down and he stood alone in the pouring rain. All was silent, but then he heard a cry, a scream of terror and pain that almost stopped his heart. Was someone lost? Trapped and in peril?

'Hello,' he cried out, cupping his hands together to help the sound to carry. 'Hello, is anyone out there?'

Again the scream rang out across the desolate moor. Someone was afraid and in terrible pain. Robert ran around, blindly trying to detect the source of the sound, which seemed to come from everywhere at once. Only when he found his feet sinking into the sodden ground did he turn and retrace his steps. He stood on the road, shaking with the cold and fear, when as suddenly as they had begun, the screams stopped.

'Hello,' he shouted. 'Please tell me where you are. Then I can help you.'

All at once, he was overcome by a terror the likes of which he had never known before, and he knew beyond a shadow of doubt that there was no-one in danger out there on the moor. That the whole thing was a trap, to lure him from the safety of the path to his death. He turned to run but fear held him tight in its grip, and then he felt a hot breath on the back of his neck and heard a voice that made his blood run cold.

'Robert!' the voice whispered in his ear. *'Robert, help me!'*

'No!' screamed Robert, his hands reaching out to cover his ears. 'You're not real! You can't be real, you're dead. I know you're dead!'

Still the whispering continued, breathy and low, as though it was inside his own head.

'Help me!' the voice implored.

Robert closed his eyes tightly and when he opened them, he looked straight into the eyes of his dead comrade. The dull, vacant eyes of a man he had watched die.

'You could have saved me, Lance Corporal,' said the shade mournfully.

Robert was suddenly overcome by such feelings of evil and loathing that he turned on his heel and ran. The wind whipped up into a frenzy and the rain was torrential. An overhead clap of thunder boomed like an explosion directly above him, and he whimpered as he ran blindly into the storm.

The soldier was sure he had never before felt such fear. That terror had never held him quite so tightly in its grip, as it did now. He was a brave man, he knew it! But against the unknown? Things he could neither cause harm to or protect himself from. Things that, until that very night, he had no cause to give credence to.

From all around him the moor was alive with screeching and howling, and somewhere deep in the back of his mind, an evil sniggering voice taunted him as he ran.

'You could have helped me, Robert...'

Robert burst into the waiting room as if the devil himself were chasing him, and seeing the expression on his face, his fellow travellers wouldn't be wrong in believing it to be so. Everyone jumped as he fell through the door and onto his knees, soaked and panting after his ordeal. The professor was the first to run over to the soldier and help him to his feet.

'S-sorry folks,' Robert managed to stammer breathlessly. 'I co— I couldn't get halfway across the moor without the storm d-driving me back.'

'Well, that's that, then,' said Sir Gregory and slumped down as though wearily resigned to his fate. He took out his pipe. 'Nothing more a fellow can do.'

The ladies fussed over Robert, pulling him up a chair by the fire and hanging his wet coat off the back of another to dry. Arthur came back in with towels and a steaming mug of tea, which the soldier accepted gratefully.

'Any news?' Robert said, nodding at the wireless.

The people in the waiting room looked at one another nervously.

'We're in for one hell of a night, my friend,' said Travers from the chimney corner.

'Hmm!' said Sir Gregory through his pipe and nothing more.

'Let's make the best of a bad situation then,' said the professor, standing to poke the fire.

'It's an intolerable situation,' grunted Sir Gregory. 'My wife and I are quite unused to—'

'Be quiet Gregory dear! I haven't seen this much excitement since the King's funeral.' Lady Agnes walked back to her seat from where she'd been tending to the soldier, whose teeth had not stopped chattering since his return. Gregory looked up at his wife in shock, and Ellen grinned at Robert. It was obvious the woman had never stood up to her domineering husband before.

'I could check and see if the way up to the house is clear. I'm sure the ladies would be more comfortable there,' cut in Arthur. 'But the river is fast-flowing at the best of times and if it's swollen, it could easily have taken the rickety old bridge with it.'

Sir Gregory was about to reply, but a stern look from his wife silenced him.

'That's very kind of you, Stationmaster.' Lady Agnes smiled warmly.

'Please, call me Arthur.'

Arthur shivered as he stepped out onto the platform. The soldier had returned without his torch and Arthur hadn't pursued the matter. It was an old torch anyway, and he always kept a spare in his office. This he carried with him now. Though little good it did in lighting his way out here.

This certainly is a freak storm, he thought to himself.

A storm of this ferocity would normally blow itself out within an hour. This had been building up all day and seemed set to rage all night. What had the weather report said? A cluster of storms. The wind and rain beat at his face and head, and he rubbed his eyes to clear his vision.

He needed to relight the up platform lamps before anything else. He would have done it sooner had he realised they were out. He completed the task quickly, feeling strangely vulnerable. Try as he might, he could not shake off the impression of being watched. He supposed it to be the nervousness of the passengers, rubbing off on him. Finally, he set off to the rear of the station where his house was situated.

He didn't fancy taking the bridge, so he crossed the line, knowing that he wasn't in any danger from oncoming trains. Even being in his own territory, he felt, oddly enough for a practical man of his years, exposed, and he could easily imagine how the soldier might feel lost and disorientated out there on the open moor.

Once on the down platform, he thought he saw movement from the corner of his eye, over by the goods sheds. When he looked again, there was nothing amiss.

'Pull yourself together, Arthur,' he said. 'The storm's playing tricks with your mind is all.'

When he reached the sheds, he decided to take a quick look around to satisfy his curiosity and check that all was well. Although barely audible, amid the wailing of the storm he could just about hear a creaking and groaning as the padlocked doors of the outbuildings strained against the full force of the wind. There was no lighting at the back of the station, and the hulking form of the goods sheds was silhouetted against the stormy wind-tossed clouds, as the skies were bathed in lightning flare. Soon enough all was plunged into darkness.

'Bloody hell,' said Arthur, shining his torch about and taking a quick look around. He wished the passengers had not been stranded at his station. A bit of supper and a stiff brandy by the fire with his dog and the wireless before bed would be just what the doctor ordered. Instead, he was stuck at the station listening to that bloody KC and his constant moaning.

He'd recognised the whining old sod from the newspaper. Hadn't he recently received recognition for sending that kidnapper to the gallows? Arthur shuddered. Horrible business that. For what that bastard had done to that little boy, he deserved to swing. Barnes was right about that.

He stepped out from the shelter of the sheds, and an almighty gust of wind threatened to blow him clean off his feet.

'Bloody hell,' he repeated, startled by the ferocity, his hand shaking as he held onto his torch. It was colder than was natural for early autumn, that was for sure.

He walked up the narrow path that led to the bridge and home and groaned with dismay at the sight that greeted him. The bridge and most of the bank had been washed away, and the water level was still rising.

'Oh no,' he groaned. 'No, no!'

He imagined he could hear his dog howling in the house, but it could only have been the wind. He walked closer to the river, and he could see the debris of the old bridge and other detritus had become wedged between the two banks and were forming a dam, the water building up on one side at an alarming rate. There was no danger to his home, but if it carried on swelling at this level, there may well be some damage to the sheds and their equipment.

He looked around in desperation. Should he go back to the waiting room and ask the soldier and the other young gentleman to help him clear the debris? No, he couldn't risk placing passengers in harm's way, and he knew there would be no-one else around who could help him, with the signalman unable to leave his box.

'Think man, think!' he scolded himself. 'Old Albert would've known what to do.'

At the thought of his father, he was filled, as he often was, with feelings of guilt and remorse. He quickly brushed them aside and tried to think. Down by the sheds he had spotted an old wooden prop with a hooked end. He knew the gangers sometimes used them to clear debris from the track. He walked back to the outbuildings and grabbed the stick from its resting place

If only I can knock at least some of the top clear, he thought, the water could flow a little easier. It wasn't much but it was all he had.

Taking the prop in his free hand, he walked carefully toward the water's edge. Once or twice he almost slipped in the mud, quickly regaining his balance by leaning on the stick.

He squatted, feet apart, on the bank close to the dam, and once he was sure of his balance, he took the flat end of the prop and began poking at the looser debris at the top. One or two small planks from the footbridge came loose, and he guided them towards the bank at his feet and plucked them out, kneeling on one but careful not to lean too far over.

He tried again, but the dam was tightly wedged and wouldn't budge, so he turned the prop around, and taking the hooked side, he wrapped it around a protruding branch halfway down the dam wall.

'If only I can get some good leverage on this, I might get the whole thing to topple,' he thought aloud. He pulled firmly, but the branch wouldn't budge. Keeping one hand on the ground for balance, he pulled a little harder, and the branch moved a fraction. He tried to unhook the prop to grab the wood a little further down, but it was stuck.

'Aaargh!' he cried out in frustration. The wind was screaming past his ears, and the rain ferociously beat at his face and head.

Suddenly, he saw something moving through the water, something small, pink, and fleshy looking. He stood, and pushing against the firmly tethered prop for extra support, he leaned forward slightly to get a better view.

A hand the size of a small child's broke the water and seemed to reach for him. In alarm he pulled back, tugging at the stick as he did so. Was there a child drowned in the river? It didn't bear thinking about. All of a sudden, the prop broke free, leaving the hook embedded in the branch. Arthur lost his footing and slid on the muddy verge. Unable to stop himself, he plunged into the turbulent waters, an impromptu gasp of shock forcing him to swallow the foul, murky liquid.

He grabbed blindly for the branch, catching his hand on the jagged edge. A sharp piece of debris broke away from the dam, cutting him deeply above the eye. As the water filled his mouth, there was a burning sensation in his throat. He felt a little lightheaded, and the sensation was not unpleasant. He managed to get his head above water and took a deep, gasping breath. The hand! The child's hand. Taking another deep breath and without any fear for his own safety, he plunged back under. The waters were calmer below, but visibility was poor. He shuddered as hands reached out and caressed him as he passed, knowing it was merely vegetation, the feeling unpleasant, nonetheless. He searched but could find no trace of the child's body. It couldn't have been carried upstream, against the current, and with the dam blocking the way ahead there was nowhere for it to go.

Finally satisfied there was no child in those muddy, swirling waters, and with his lungs fit to burst, he swam to the surface. He was a considerable distance from the bank, station side, and found himself to have swum away from the dam, but the current was strong, so he was drifting ever closer.

He was tiring, weak. His limbs felt leaden. He never had been a strong swimmer, but maybe holding onto the dam for purchase, he could edge his way over to the bank.

Closer now. Treading water to stay afloat, he could almost reach out and touch the dam. All of a sudden, something had hold of him. Something was grabbing his leg, trying to drag his head under. He panicked and kicked out wildly, his heart hammering in his chest, the roaring of the water deafening in his ears. He lashed out once more and felt something give, and suddenly he was free.

He surfaced and his outstretched hand brushed against something rough. The dam! Taking a firm hold, he pulled himself along until he could feel the hard standing, struggling to find his feet, slipping on the slimy mud and plant life on the riverbed before gaining a firmer footing.

He finally reached the bank and clambered out, his progress slow and difficult. He crawled through the mud to the firmer grassy verge, collapsing in a heap, his breathing laboured, his chest tight and painful. He gasped for air and coughed, spitting out the foul-tasting muddy water in his mouth. He wiped blood from the gash above his eye and waited for his breathing to ease, shivering with cold and shock.

It would have been easier for him to climb out on the right bank closer to home and he looked longingly up at the house, a darkened silhouette in the distance, but he knew he had to get back to the station. He could not and would not abandon his stranded passengers.

The cut above his eye was throbbing and his hand was stinging. He had quite badly banged one knee when he fell, but other than that he was none the worse for wear. He rested for a moment longer and stared up at the sky, moonless now and angry. Then forcing himself to his feet, he staggered away from the river, towards the station.

Lightning forked above. There was a blinding flash, and he heard a loud bang as though something nearby had been struck. The air was charged with electricity, and he felt the static along the exposed skin of his hands and face.

Whether from the impetus of the strike or the natural instincts of a man having seen battle, he found himself on the ground. A flaming piece of timber whizzed past his ear, and he flinched, protectively covering his head with his arms. Visions of the Somme flashed before his eyes, and he curled into himself.

The cloying smell of smoke jolted Arthur back to the present. He gathered his wits and turned to see that the dam had collapsed. He felt his heart pounding in his chest. With moments to spare, he had escaped a lightning strike and certain death.

He carefully edged closer to the river. It was calmer now the dam no longer restricted its flow. He kicked away some of the smouldering and shattered pieces. At the water's edge, something caught his eye. A tiny glove, pink, dirty, and sodden. It floated downstream away from him.

He shuddered and tried to push all notions of it being the hand of a child firmly out of his mind.

Chapter Fifteen

'Dear God, man, what happened to you?' barked Sir Gregory on seeing Arthur come through the waiting room door.

Arthur put up a hand to reassure them, as the two women and the professor came running to meet him, their eyes wide with concern.

'Oh, you're bleeding!' cried Ellen.

'It's fine. I'm fine, really,' said Arthur. 'The bridge was out and that and other debris had formed a dam. I fell in trying to clear it so the goods sheds wouldn't flood.'

'Why, my dear fellow,' said the professor, 'why didn't you ask one of us for help?'

'Really, I'm fine,' said Arthur, embarrassed by all the attention. 'I have fresh clothes in my office. If you'll excuse me, I'll dry off in there and change.'

After collecting fresh towels and filling a bowl from the kettle in the kitchen, he limped into his office and made up a good fire from the idling coals in the grate. The kindling soon caught on, and he relished the welcoming sight of a living flame. It was to be expected to feel a chill after the soaking he'd had, and also that it should be cold out on the stormy moor at this late hour, whatever the season. But as Arthur huddled closer to the fire, he thought again how the evening had been unseasonably cold, even inside the station. And how even before his *little* accident, there had been occasions over the last few hours when he had felt himself chilled to the marrow.

After removing his wet clothes and checking for cuts and bruises, he bathed his eye and his hand and patched them up with dressings from his first aid kit. The cut above his eye would probably need to be stitched, but for now this would have to do. He cleaned himself up as best he could and changed into fresh, dry clothes and was about to take a nip of whiskey to keep the cold at bay when a piercing scream from next door sent him running into the waiting room.

There, in the middle of the floor, in a dead faint with her head on her husband's knee, lay Lady Agnes.

The waiting room had been quiet again. Sir Gregory was engrossed in a crossword, the professor seemed to be sleeping, and the soldier was wrapped in his own thoughts. The two ladies had sat together in silence, Lady Agnes comforted by the close proximity of the younger woman. Arthur, of course, was next door, changing in his office.

Travers stood up and walked around the waiting room to stretch his legs. Robert watched him from his seat. There was something shifty about the man he couldn't quite put his finger on. Travers stood behind Ellen, leaned in close, and began to speak in hushed tones.

'Oh!' said Ellen, turning sharply and looking at the man. Travers straightened up with a smile, and the soldier watched him as he made his way to his seat. A loud clap of thunder overhead made everyone jump and woke the professor with a start.

Lady Agnes was, all of a sudden, very cold, and she pulled her coat tightly around her shoulders. She had the feeling she was being watched and looked nervously around the room, noticing how quiet everything had become.

A flash of lightening made her look toward the window. There, an obscure figure stood outside on the platform watching the people within. The figure of a man. Just a tall silhouette, set against a blanched and stricken sky, and then, the lightning faded away to nothing. From the dim illumination of the room, Lady Agnes could just about make out a face. A pale, haunted face that held her enrapt, drawn to the dark shadowy voids where his eyes should be. She froze, certain that her heart would stop in terror. She closed her eyes tight and prayed silently, her quivering mouth forming words that no-one else could hear. When she opened her eyes again, the figure had gone, and that was when she screamed and fell to the floor in a faint. Her husband and Ellen ran to her aid. The professor stood in alarm.

From the dark chimney corner, Robert heard a low snigger. 'What did he say to you?' he demanded of Ellen, striding past the prostrate figure of Lady Agnes. 'What did that creature say to you?'

Ellen gasped.

'I hardly think this is the right time,' added the professor, looking over to where the soldier stood. 'Poor Lady Agnes, is she…'

Suddenly Arthur came into the room and saw Lady Agnes on the floor. By now she was stirring, moaning. She regained consciousness and looked up at the people crowded around her.

'Give her room,' said Arthur. 'She's fainted. She needs air.'

Lady Agnes recovered her wits, and her eyes widened with fear as she grabbed her husband's arm tightly.

'The man,' she mumbled. 'On the platform… He stared in at me, but he… He had no eyes! Oh Gregory, it was awful. Awful!'

She started to sob, and Gregory put a protective arm around his wife to comfort her. Arthur ran to the door to check outside on the platform, and Robert made to follow him when Ellen grabbed his arm forcefully. Both looked towards the shadowy chimney corner, where only the bottom of Travers' legs and feet were visible. Then Ellen turned to Robert, her eyes aglow in the light of the fire.

'What did he say to you, Miss?' Robert said, his face set hard. Ellen looked up at him, with his ruggedly handsome face, his wide jaw and deep-set eyes. He reminded her of Humphrey Bogart.

'Please, call me Ellen.'

'And I'm Robert.'

'I think he believes me to be a fool, Robert,' said Ellen. 'But I'm afraid he'll find me neither gullible nor easily scared.'

The professor and Sir Gregory lifted Lady Agnes to her feet and seated her by the fire, the latter making gentle cooing sounds to calm his fearful wife.

A stark contrast to the gruff and haughty exterior displayed earlier in the evening, Ellen thought, turning her attention to Lady Agnes once more. A hush descended upon those gathered in the waiting room, a loud crack from a spitting coal causing the elders seated closest to the fire to jump in fright.

'What did he say to you?' the soldier repeated.

Ellen turned to face him, looking briefly at Travers before moving closer to whisper in the soldier's ear.

'He told me the station was haunted.'

His fiancée had never looked so beautiful. He watched her with a warm feeling inside as she sipped her tea and chattered excitedly about flowers and rings... and honeymoons. A frown wrinkled his brow when he considered the cost of keeping his beloved happy, but she was too preoccupied to notice.

He thought how child-like she looked with her shining eyes and her incessant giggles, and he knew then that he would do anything to make her dreams come true. To buy her the matching rings she so desired, the honeymoon in Venice or Paris. He left her to her society magazines and afternoon tea, kissed her lightly on the cheek, and with a heavy heart, walked over to the bank.

Nervous Norman, fidgety as ever, had been pacing the banking hall looking for him when he returned. Mrs Baxter was waiting for him, and she would see no-one else. He smiled, knowing the cantankerous old dear had a soft spot for him, also knowing that she would be adding to her immense wealth by depositing into her account. He had been siphoning the odd copper from several of his wealthier clientele for the past few months now and transferring the money into a dummy account. A few bob here and there, never enough to be missed. But so far, probably due to her fondness for him, he'd avoided doing so to Mrs Baxter's account, even though she was one of the richest people in town.

His was a pretty little town, close to the sea with far-reaching views and surrounded by farmland and lush green fields. It was a haven for the retired wealthy of Harrogate and York, and with many of London's elite having their country pile close by, he had his choice of rich pickings.

Mrs Baxter, who'd received a substantial amount after the death of her late husband in an industrial accident, was also in benefit of a tidy pension each week. Add this to rent she received from inherited properties, and Mrs Baxter was a very wealthy lady indeed. In fact, that very afternoon she was in town to deposit a cheque for the substantial amount of one hundred and two pounds and ten shillings, two shillings of which found its way into the account of her favourite bank clerk.

Chapter Sixteen

'Bloody ghosts!' snapped Arthur. 'That's all we need with people already shaken. What's the fellow thinking of?'

Accompanied by the soldier, Arthur was checking the station platforms and outbuildings following Lady Agnes' sighting of the intruder.

'I'm not sure,' Robert replied angrily. 'But someone needs to have a word.'

'Right now, I'm more concerned about a trespasser on railway property.'

'I thought I saw someone, too,' Robert told the stationmaster. 'When I set out to Hubery. Down there by the tracks.'

Arthur looked at him in disbelief.

'Of course, I couldn't be sure! It was dark and it is easy to become irrational out here, given the circumstances,' the soldier replied a little sheepishly, realising he should probably have informed the stationmaster sooner.

'Hmmm!' said the railway man, frowning.

'Naturally I called out! But when I received no reply, I thought it must be my eyes playing tricks on me. The platform was full of shadows.'

'If you could check the toilet block and the storerooms…' Arthur replied curtly, handing him the keys. 'I'll check over by the sheds.'

Lady Agnes could not be persuaded that she hadn't indeed encountered a ghost. Even after a shot of brandy and hot, sweet tea, she stood by her conviction. There was no doubt in her mind that the creature who watched her from the platform was 'not of this world.' Her husband, over the shock of her little fainting spell, had scoffed and ridiculed the notion. Ellen too had tried to calm the nervous old lady, and the professor had attempted to convince Lady Agnes that there was no scientific evidence as to prove the existence of spirits. Nor was there any evidence whatsoever to suggest that the man on the platform was anything but a prowler looking to shelter from the storm.

Ellen was not primarily concerned with Lady Agnes' tale of the supernatural, more worried for the old lady's well-being. She kept looking around nervously at the man in the corner, and although his face was in shadow, she was certain he was grinning at her. His behaviour thus far was certainly odd, and truth be known, Ellen found the man rather unpleasant. She shuddered and went over to the window to look for the men returning. She hoped it would be soon. Travers gave her the creeps, and she held little faith in the abilities of the professor and Sir Gregory to protect the ladies in case of an emergency.

Eventually Arthur and Robert returned, perplexed and a little uneasy. There was no-one to be found on or around the station, and unless you had keys to the outbuildings, which Arthur had just taken receipt of from the soldier, there was nowhere to hide, unless you ran along the tracks, and only a fool would do so. No, they were convinced the figure had been the result of an overwrought lady with a vivid imagination, neither man conceding their true thoughts on the matter but both willing to admit that Lady Agnes had struck them as neither overwrought nor given to flights of fancy.

It was decided in light of recent happenings, namely Lady Agnes' unfortunate encounter with a prowler, that no-one was to go wandering around the station alone. Staff conveniences were made available to the stranded passengers, the doors were locked, and Robert, Arthur, and Travers (whom the soldier kept a good eye on) took it in turns to patrol the station. After a round of toast courtesy of Arthur, and another hot drink, this one laced with a tot for good measure, the three elders dozed off to the dreamy sounds of Jack Payne and His Orchestra. It was getting late, and the BBC's programmes were drawing to a close. Sir Gregory snored softly, and from the way Lady Agnes cried out occasionally, it was obvious her sleep was troubled.

Ellen remained uneasy and kept looking over at Robert, who gave her a reassuring smile from time to time. Arthur massaged his injured knee, which guaranteed to be stiff and bruised come morning.

The storm seemed to be passing over; only the occasional flicker of lightning illuminated the waiting room windows, making diamonds of the raindrops on the glass. The wind had died down too, but the steady patter of rain persisted, and Arthur was worried about the extent of the damage the storm had wrought.

Ellen felt her eyelids growing heavy and could hardly keep them from closing. She had barely nodded off when a strange mewling sound from by the fire woke her up. It was Sir Gregory; he was whimpering and moaning in his sleep and seemed very distressed. Lady Agnes, at his side, was also roused by her husband's noise. Only the professor slept on unawares.

Sir Gregory's face was bathed in sweat, and beneath his tightly closed lids, his eyes darted about in rapid movement. He was mumbling something now, repeating himself over and over, his voice getting louder as he thrashed about in his seat.

'No!' he cried out. 'No, it's not true. He deserved to hang…He was guilty, I tell you, guilty…'

'Gregory. Gregory dear, wake up. You're dreaming. Wake up.' His wife shook his shoulder gently, afraid to startle him, but he wouldn't wake.

'I'm sorry,' said his wife to the others. 'He's been doing this lately. He's been under a lot of stress, what with the trial and all. I'm really sorry.'

All of a sudden, the old man's eyes snapped open, wide and full of fear. His wife was filled with concern, but she also looked embarrassed and irritated by the spectacle.

'Gregory, you've been dreaming again,' she chided. 'You really should see a doctor.'

The old man was groggy and looked with bleary eyes at the concerned faces of his fellow passengers. He rubbed his face vigorously before turning to his wife.

'Don't be ridiculous woman. Since when did a dream ever harm anyone?' he snapped.

Lady Agnes looked at her husband coldly, and the others turned away, embarrassed to have witnessed the quarrel between husband and wife. All but Travers, who called out from his secluded nook.

'Interesting case that, Sir Gregory.'

All eyes turned to the disembodied voice in the darkened corner. Travers stepped out of the shadows.

'What? What's that?' puffed the old man.

His wife looked at him sharply, and the professor noticed a look of alarm flicker in her eyes.

'I was in the public gallery that day, sir. That day you donned your sentencing cap and sealed that poor idiot boy's fate… *Sir!*

'What impertinence is this, my good fellow?' bellowed the judge. 'I suggest you sit down, sir, before I'm forced to take my belt to you.'

Robert stood up, ready to lunge at Travers, who calmly walked up and stood behind Ellen's seat, holding on to the backrest with both hands. If he was afraid of a beating, he certainly didn't show it. Ellen visibly shuddered at the close proximity.

'The kidnapping of that society boy, all of six he was,' Travers continued, moving around closer, his eyes never leaving the judge, who stared back incredulously. 'His mother was never allowed to identify his little body. Or what was left of it…'

Ellen looked up at Travers in horror. Lady Agnes stifled a sob.

'Why you…' said Robert, moving closer to the man.

'*Animal!*' roared Sir Gregory, red in the face and panting with exertion. 'The boy's father paid that scoundrel his ransom demands and still he tore that poor child limb from limb.'

'Oh!' cried out Lady Agnes, burying her face in her hands.

'And yet we're meant to believe that a simple stable hand engineered the whole thing?' Travers continued. 'That he single-handedly hatched an ingenious, untraceable kidnap plot, stole the boy away from home...'

'Really, this is too much,' said the professor, but Travers persisted undeterred.

'That he calculated a ransom, tactically arranged a drop-off so the police couldn't find him, callously murdered a child he had known since birth, and then calmly went back to working in the stables at the parents' home, even though he was now rich beyond his wildest dreams?'

Sir Gregory appeared to have shrunk back into himself. He seemed to find it hard to gather his words.

'It was because the boy knew him, you see?' he said imploringly to Arthur. 'That's how he was able to lead him away.' He turned to the professor. 'The boy trusted him,' he said, grabbing the professor's arm.

The judge was sweating now. He turned to look at the faces of the people around him, a sea of faces, and he felt as though he was drowning, finding it hard to breathe.

'That's enough now,' said Arthur authoritatively, grabbing Travers' arm. Travers pulled away with a strength that amazed Arthur.

'Besides,' whimpered Sir Gregory, barely audible, 'the boy's bloodied shoe was found in the stables. The evidence was irrefutable.'

'The evidence was planted by a corrupt and incompetent police force who knew there would be a public outcry if no-one was brought to trial for this atrocity,' said Travers calmly. 'You knew, Sir Gregory. You knew this and you buried it. You knew witnesses for the defence were being intimidated, and you did nothing.'

'Stop it!' groaned his wife. 'Please, stop it.'

'*Lies!*' screamed the judge, standing and roughly pushing his accuser away. 'All lies, damn you!' He shook a finger in Travers' face. His eyes were bloodshot, and his lip was trembling. 'You've no proof of this, sir, I tell you. No proof! Who the devil are you? And how can you make such outlandish claims?'

He walked away from the group, towards the back of the room and down the corridor that led to the staff conveniences. All turned and watched him go.

'Michael Turner was an innocent man, Sir Gregory! A scapegoat,' Travers called after him sadly. 'You knew it and yet you sent a poor, simple-minded man to the gallows.'

Little Hubery Station stood isolated on the sodden and storm-tossed moor. Its flickering fire-lit windows stood out like a beacon against the ravaged landscape of the dark and desolate heath.

Cut off from civilisation by a raging storm, the five passengers sat in silence. The sixth, Sir Gregory, had not yet returned from the WC after his altercation with the man, Travers.

Each one of them was encompassed in his or her own thoughts, isolated each from the other by a deep brooding introspection that hovered over them like a noxious cloud. An external entity that bored its way into the mind of its captive audience, planting in each suggestions, just seeds, ideas that germinated and grew into a dark and worrisome cognisance.

Robert was thinking, what the hell was that, and how and why had it come about? He looked across at Travers and wondered about the strange, disagreeable man. Why suddenly turn against the judge like that? He was no fan of the pompous old fool himself, less so if the accusations against him were true, but why had he been held to trial like that? An ironic turnabout for a magistrate. Travers had barely spoken two words to anyone all night and now this! It was a strange business.

Travers, who hadn't moved since sitting back in his seat, turned his head slowly towards Robert as though reading his thoughts. The soldier could feel the other man's eyes boring into him, even though Travers' face was hidden, in shadow, and Robert could feel his flesh creeping as if something were crawling on his skin, inside his clothes.

He remembered how he'd felt out there, exposed on the moor. How vulnerable he'd felt. He never wanted to feel that way again.

There was a strange, unpleasant atmosphere in the waiting room, and he was sure it was emanating from Travers. He stood and lit a cigarette and walked over to the fire.

He could see out of the corner of his eye that Ellen was watching him, and he offered her a cigarette. She accepted and came and joined him by the hearth.

She studied Robert's face in profile. The light from the fire cast deep shadows and made his features seem all the more rugged and chiselled.

'Completely the opposite of George,' she thought, 'fair, quiet and bookish.'

The soldier, Robert, was dark and mysterious. If only she knew what was troubling him. Ellen always thought herself very perceptive when it came to others. She watched as he drew from his cigarette, causing the end to glow like a headlamp. She found herself wondering whether he was married. Who was waiting for him anxiously at home? What was his wife like? Did they have children?

She glanced at the insignia on his arm. What kind of a man was the lance corporal? Was he a good soldier? Had he ever killed anyone?

Hidden among the shadows in the darkened chimney corner, Travers smiled.

Lady Agnes was thinking, he couldn't know that. He simply couldn't! What was the wretched man's idea? Was it some kind of blackmail plot? Was it his intention to bring her husband down? Defame him? Maybe he was someone Gregory had previously sent to prison, or the family member of someone he'd sent there.

Perhaps he was related to that poor soul Gregory had sent to the gallows. But how could he know about the evidence? Why here, and now? How did he know they would be here? How could he? Had he followed them?

At that last thought, she began trembling uncontrollably. The professor, sat next to her, looked at her with concern.

'Oh dear, where is my husband?' she said out loud.

Arthur tried to phone Shearing's Vale to see whether there had been any progress, but it seemed the storm had brought the phone lines down. Only the same static he'd heard earlier on the wireless came from the instrument. He placed the receiver back onto its cradle and sat on the edge of his desk, rubbing his eyes.

'Oh, let this night be over,' he groaned. 'Let it be over.'

He thought of what had just happened and how strange the man, Travers, was. Earlier, after checking the station buildings, Arthur learned a little about the soldier, Robert, and how he had finished serving in India and was to be stationed at Catterick. He'd had a good conversation with the young lady, Ellen, as the two of them made tea, about how she was to be department head at a girls' school in Northumberland, and about Sir Gregory everyone was already familiar. Besides, his wife, Lady Agnes, had been pleasant and talkative for most of the evening. The professor, they'd learned, was unmarried and lived in Saltburn and was travelling home from visiting friends in Cambridge, but about Travers, they knew nothing. He had made no attempts to communicate nor offered any information about himself to anyone.

'Very odd,' thought Arthur. 'Very, very odd.' He felt the onset of a bad headache and massaged his temples. 'At least the storm is calming somewhat, for now… in fact it's almost too quiet!' he mused.

He stood and was about to make for the door when the phone sprang into life, its shrill ringing deafening in the lull of the storm.

'Bloody hell!' he exclaimed, and then, 'Oh, thank God for small mercies.' He grabbed the receiver. 'Little Hubery. Stationmaster McLaren speaking.'

Static, a voice barely discernible, more static and then…

'Arthur? Arthur…'

It couldn't be! It sounded like his father, long gone now.

'Hello. Hello? Yes?' Suddenly his blood ran cold as a low snigger could be heard over the phone and then the voice on the other end wound down, became deeper, low and drawn out. It was the same voice he'd heard on the wireless earlier. And it issued Arthur the same ominous warning.

'Before this night ends…'

Sir Gregory washed his face and looked at himself in the mirror. His heart was racing and he had a pain across his shoulder. His breath was laboured, and fury and loathing coursed through his veins like a poison.

'Damned fellow,' he cursed. To attack him like that, in front of his wife, in front of all those people. Why, if he were twenty years younger, he'd thrash the scoundrel to within an inch of his life. What did he hope to achieve?

He felt a darkness creep into his mind, crawling, probing, seeking out his deepest thoughts, searching for and merging with the wickedness in his own soul. His thoughts turned inward, heinous thoughts. Thoughts of harming, of silencing for good this filth that sought to challenge, to expose him. The judge was a man of some influence. Who did this malefactor think he was? This judge of judges. Sir Gregory winced as a pain shot up his arm and his chest tightened.

'*Lies!*' he hissed at his reflection. '*All lies!*'

Who was Gregory to accuse the chief of police? He held no sway over the force and what they did or didn't do. So what if they *had* tampered with the evidence? How was that *his* fault? Besides the jury convicted Turner. Not he, himself. The judge had merely passed sentence, and the jury, well, could only work with what they had... the evidence against the boy was overwhelming... if he *was* innocent then...

A sudden movement among the shadows at the back of the room caught his attention. He wiped his face on the towel and made to turn around when something drew him to the mirror. Over his left shoulder, he could see a figure, that of a young man, wiry and strong with foppish, dark hair. The figure was looking down at the ground, and the judge found himself paralysed with fear, unable to tear his gaze away from the reflection of the boy who even now raised his head to meet him eye to eye.

Sir Gregory wheezed and fought for breath. Beads of sweat covered his forehead; the back of his neck felt hot and clammy. He felt as if he were burning, even though the room itself seemed icy cold. His legs refused to support him, and he managed to grab the edge of the sink for stability.

The boy's face was in full view now, and the judge closed his eyes tightly. He didn't need to look. He already knew that this was the shade of Michael Turner, the boy he had sent to the gallows, and he was here to exact his deadly revenge. He knew this with all the certainty of a dying man, and he knew his time was near. He was, after all, a man of justice, and this was to be his trial and justice would now be served. A tear squeezed its way from between his tightly closed lids, and he felt certain he would have to meet Turner's ghost face to face, man to man.

If he expected rattling chains and lamentations, then the judge was mistaken, for the shade of Michael Turner stood before him now as the boy had done in life. The look of terror he had last worn was replaced by that of melancholy and resignation, as though the spirit felt no satisfaction in what was about to happen

Dark rings circled his eyes, and his lips and cheek were bloodless, almost translucent. He wore the same clothes he had worn when sentencing was passed, and he never once took his eyes off Sir Gregory.

'What do you want of me, spirit?' Gregory asked with all of the false bravado of Scrooge when faced with Marley's ghost. The boy's lips moved but no words came out. He opened his mouth wide, and it was cavernous, empty and black, just a dark void, without tongue or teeth. The judge felt as though he were being pulled in, as though the very soul were being sucked from him, and then as suddenly as it had appeared, the spirit was gone.

Sir Gregory sank to his knees and somehow managed to pull his legs around so his back rested against the pedestal of the sink. The pain in his chest had subsided, and his breathing seemed to have eased. He felt as though he were floating, no longer grounded. Had he been spared?

He could hear the sounds around him. He could hear someone calling out to him, pounding on the door, which he was certain wasn't locked, but all the sounds were distant, as if muted by time. He tried to call out but found *himself* muted by fear.

Then he heard from the corner of the room a strange sound, like a death rattle in someone's throat, and then a low, sinister chuckle. He felt, all of a sudden, numb, no longer registering hot or cold, and he could see the shadows moving before his eyes like living forms. He heard his own voice cry out '*death by hanging*!' but it didn't come from within.

He could just about make out movement from the far corner, where the shadows were deepest, and his eyes bulged with terror at the sight before him. He felt a rope being placed around his neck. Rough and chaffing against his clammy skin, the hangman's knot unyielding against the vertebrae of his neck.

And then it tightened and the floor beneath him seemed to shift and fall away.

His fingers grasped frantically at his collar, but there was nothing there and he felt once more the pedestal of the sink firm against his back. Still the old man struggled for breath. His throat felt constricted, his windpipe crushed, and his tongue lolled lifelessly from his mouth. He felt the hot liquid run down his inner thigh and heard the sound of a gavel hitting a sounding block.

The last thing Sir Gregory ever saw was the lipless mouth of the hanging carcass grinning at him from the corner of the room.

Chapter Nineteen

Professor Victor Rose walked with some apprehension down the darkened corridor toward the staff conveniences. Not easily given to tales of ghosts and ghouls and things that go bump in the night, he had to admit to feeling rather spooked, what with the storm, the wild moorland setting, talk of prowlers, and now this... this creepy man, Travers.

What was his game, he wondered, and what was the meaning of that outburst? Could his accusations be true? Sir Gregory had clearly been shaken by it.

He was going at the request of Lady Agnes to check on the judge. Her husband had been gone a while and she was getting worried. The professor, normally a level-headed man, crossed his fingers and hoped for no more unpleasant surprises that night.

When he reached the door, his apprehension deepened and he paused for a moment, his fingertips resting lightly against the wood. He put his ear to the panel and listened. He could hear faint murmurs of conversation from the other passengers in the waiting room. Arthur was in his office, presumably trying the telephone again, and Professor Rose could see a chink of light beneath the office door. From within the staff toilet, all was quiet, but shadows stirring beneath the door told the professor that Barnes was moving about.

'Sir Gregory?' The professor tapped gently on the door and then knocked a little louder. 'Sir Gregory, are you all right? Your wife is quite concerned about you.' He pushed against the door, but it wouldn't budge.

'Strange,' he thought to himself. 'I don't remember the outer door having a lock!'

'Sir Gregory, could you open the door please?' From inside, he thought he heard laughter, deep and rasping. He pushed the door firmly, but it held fast.

'Sir Gregory, please. If you can hear me, open the door.'

The professor spoke a little louder, but not loud enough to cause concern to the judge's wife, sitting in the waiting room down the corridor. He put his shoulder against the door and applied some force, but still it refused to move. He could hear Sir Gregory talking to someone and wondered if he'd caught the prowler. The thought left the professor cold, and he shook the door so hard that the doorknob rattled. Suddenly, the talking stopped, and he stood back to gain momentum to charge, when all at once the door of the stationmaster's office swung open.

'Arthur,' the professor hissed at the surprised man. 'The key to this door, do you have it? I fear Sir Gregory is trapped inside.'

'That door doesn't lock,' said the stationmaster with a puzzled expression. 'It's recently planed, it doesn't even stick.'

'Then please,' cried Professor Rose, 'help me open it.'

Arthur grabbed the doorknob and gave it a twist. It turned easily and the door swung open. The two men looked at each other in bewilderment for a moment and then rushed inside. There on the floor, leant against the pedestal of the sink, sprawled Sir Gregory. His jaw drooped and the tongue lolled from between the man's blue-tinged lips like meat hanging from a butcher's hook. Saliva moistened his chin, and his wide eyes fixed upon the darkened corner by the cubicle, where shadows cast by the gas lamp seemed to all but vanish into the impenetrable blackness of the deep recess.

The judge's pupils were dilated, only the tiniest rim of grey-flecked iris was visible. Sir Gregory was dead.

'Good Lord,' gasped the professor. 'Look at his face!'

'God help us,' Arthur said, quickly looking away. Then he turned to the professor and his expression was gravely serious. 'It looks to me, Professor Rose,' he said, 'as though this man died of fright!'

Back in the waiting room, Arthur, the professor, and Robert stood deep in conversation, their faces sombre. Above the hushed exchange, the occasional sob rang out from Lady Agnes, who was being given brandy and comforted by Ellen; the latter kept looking up at the men with nervous curiosity. Sir Gregory's body had been removed to a small room at the back of the building and covered with a fire blanket. Arthur had again attempted, unsuccessfully, to use the phone, and Travers had been ordered not to leave his seat. The wireless was broadcasting the news prior to the shipping forecast, and Ellen moved to turn it off.

'Leave it on, dear,' sniffed Lady Agnes, dabbing her eyes with a lace handkerchief. 'It comforts me.'

'What if the man died as a direct result of Travers' confrontation?' said Robert.

'We can't possibly know that,' replied Arthur. 'Besides, it looks for all intents and purposes as if he had a heart attack.'

'But the expression on his face,' cried the professor. 'It was a look of sheer terror!'

'And Travers never left his seat,' Arthur said. 'He was nowhere near the man when he died. True, he may have challenged Sir Gregory. Undoubtedly, he upset him. But to have brought about his death? He wasn't even aggressive toward him. He's done nothing wrong. We would be breaking the law if we attempted to accost him in any way.'

The soldier sighed and turned angrily towards the chimney corner before looking back.

'So what do you suggest then, stationmaster?' he asked coldly. 'We are all holed up here with tales of ghosts and prowlers abounding and then there's this, this creature…'

'Please lower your voice,' said the professor. 'We don't want to upset the ladies any more than they already are. He is a little odd, I agree, but Arthur's right. We can't go locking him up against his will. Better we all stick together and keep an eye on him.'

Arthur gathered everyone around. Five weary travellers with pale faces and bloodshot eyes sat huddled around the fire. In the amber glow, Ellen's eyes were wide with trepidation, while Lady Agnes' glistened with unshed tears. The soldier and the professor were silent. Even Travers was respectfully subdued, although Robert was certain he saw a trace of mockery in his eyes. Or maybe it was just the firelight. He rubbed his own tired eyes and caught Ellen watching him from the seat opposite. She smiled half-heartedly at the man, but he never returned her smile, turning instead to look at Arthur. The stationmaster cleared his throat.

'Ladies and gentlemen, we have all suffered a terrific shock tonight, and I'm sure our thoughts and condolences lie with Lady Agnes.'

Ellen rubbed the old lady's shoulder, and Sir Gregory's widow nodded her thanks at those gathered.

'The loss of Sir Gregory is indeed tragic and in such unfortunate circumstances. However, having thoroughly examined the, err, the gentleman concerned, Professor Rose, Lance Corporal Newton and I are quite convinced that there are no signs of trauma to the body, so we can conclude that Sir Gregory died of entirely natural causes.'

Ellen found herself glaring at Travers, who met her eye and refused to look away. For a moment she was unable to break his stare, mesmerised by the bottomless depths of those pale, colourless eyes. She had never seen eyes so deep and yet so empty. It was as though they lacked humanity, they were soulless! She eventually pulled away and shuddered. She suddenly felt violated. It was as though he had been inside her mind and could see her deepest, darkest secrets. She attempted to shake off the feeling, but it stayed with her. She tried to concentrate on what Arthur was saying, but she could hear Travers' voice in her head, calling her...

'Ellen, Elllllllll-en...'

Unable to stop herself, her eyes met his again and locked. Arthur's words were faint, like background noise. All she could hear was Travers. Travers calling her. Putting images into her head. Rooting out her own thoughts and taunting her with them. Reminding her of things best forgotten. Of things that brought her shame. Of George. Of her affair, the way it ended and the people it hurt. She hadn't meant for it to happen. But she was helpless to stop it. Ellen wasn't malicious and she wasn't cruel, but she was blinded by what she believed to be love, and her actions had borne severe consequences. But how on earth could this beast, Travers, know this? Was he reading her thoughts? How and why was he doing this?

Arthur's voice cut through the mist like a scythe through wheat, bringing her abruptly back to the present. She felt exposed and suddenly very frightened. Then Travers blinked and she was able to look away. Her mouth felt dry, and her heart was pounding in her chest. Had Travers done the same thing to the judge, causing his aging heart to fail? Who was he? *What* was he, and what did he want with her?

'We believe there was a prowler on the premises earlier,' said the stationmaster.

Ellen looked at Lady Agnes with alarm.

'Probably just someone expecting the station to be empty and looking for shelter from the storm. But I don't feel that he meant us any harm and is likely as not long gone. The incident with the wireless, the static, was surely down to the storm. We are all a little tired and susceptible to influences that we wouldn't normally take mind of, but I can assure you, we are quite safe in the station.'

Arthur remembered the voice over the phone, and the cold hand of fear crept around his heart. Robert, appreciating Arthur's efforts to calm his passengers, fought to quell the feelings of 'fight or flight' rising in his breast. In the periphery of her vision, Ellen caught Travers looking at her once more, and despite the heat from the fire, she shuddered.

'I am hopeful that soon the storm will clear, you can call your families. and I can put a call through to Shearing's Vale. Maybe they can arrange for a bus, and we can get you all home…' Arthur continued.

A sob from Lady Agnes silenced him.

Chapter Twenty

'Guilt, my dears,' said Lady Agnes, 'or rather a guilty conscience, is as likely a contributory factor in my husband's death as any other. For a guilty conscience is a terrible burden, and Gregory, God rest his soul, stood guilty as charged.'

The others stared at Lady Agnes as if she'd gone mad, and the professor opened his mouth to speak, but the old lady held up a hand as if to stop him.

'The gentleman here, Mr Travers, was right in the accusation he made against him. For Gregory knew there had been a cover-up by the police, and he did nothing.'

There was a collective gasp and Robert was about to cut in when Travers silenced him.

'Please,' he implored. 'Allow the lady to finish.'

Robert glared at the man but held his tongue.

'He knew the public were baying for blood,' the old lady continued, 'and he sent that poor young man to the gallows, knowing that the guilty party roamed free. Oh, the young stable hand was involved right enough. He could not deny that he had led the kidnapper to the boy, or the boy to his kidnapper. But he was a simple-minded fellow who doted on the child, so one can assume that whatever part he played in the crime, he did so unwittingly.'

She sniffed and dabbed her eyes before carrying on.

'Gregory and Chief of Police, Thomas Grainger, had been friends for years. They went to college together, although Thomas was older than Gregory, and he and his wife, Vera, were guests at both our wedding and our son's christening. Anyhow, Thomas came to Gregory with suspicions that the evidence had been tampered with by his senior officers at The Yard. He spoke of his fears for his reputation and his livelihood if the kidnapper wasn't brought to justice. Gregory was appalled. He begged Thomas to investigate the matter, set things straight before it was too late. He even threatened to halt the trial!'

'So what happened?' said Arthur, sitting forward in his chair.

'My husband was a very loyal man, Mr McLaren. When Thomas said it had already gone too far, that there would be severe repercussions, and he felt he had no other choice but to turn a blind eye, even though he was certain his officers had tampered with the evidence…' She paused and hung her head. 'I'm afraid Gregory felt obliged to stand by him.'

The soldier scoffed.

'The police were convinced at that point that Mr Turner was involved in some way, but they felt he couldn't be the one who'd kidnapped the child. At least, not alone.'

'What?' said Robert, the disgust and disbelief evident in his voice. Lady Agnes looked up at the professor for support, but he simply shook his head. She carried on sadly.

'It's not known whether Mr Turner inadvertently allowed the kidnappers onto the property or whether he was tricked into taking the boy to them.' She sighed. 'He confessed to having been with the boy that day, in light of new evidence having surfaced. But he was very frightened and upset, his mind was muddled, and he couldn't give a clear indication of what had happened. Nor could he give a description of the others involved. It was clear, however, that he had no idea as to his participation with the 'kidnapper' or where his actions would lead.'

'Dear God!' cried Ellen.

The old lady continued. 'Michael Turner was, as Mr Travers had said, a poor simpleton, an innocent scapegoat. The police had no further leads as to the kidnapper's identity, and Mr Turner was an unreliable witness, unable to supply any clues. Perhaps he feared what the kidnappers would do to the boy if he told. Nor could he supply any clear alibi for himself.' She sighed. 'Well…'

'How did the police coerce the stable hand into admitting he'd had the child, Lady Agnes?' Ellen asked her gently. It seemed, as is the way at such times, that the kindness of the younger woman caused the old lady to break down in floods of tears.

'When the beast sent the police the boy's shoe…' She sobbed, unable to continue, and the professor offered her his handkerchief. Soon enough, she composed herself.

'When the kidnapper sent the boy's bloodied shoe to the police, a senior officer, it seems, took it upon himself to set a trap for Mr Turner. H-he planted it in the stable where the young man worked. The hand had no other choice than to admit that he had been with the child and that they had met with another party. Other than that, he would or perhaps could say no more. As the police suspected that the boy was still alive at that time and that Michael Turner could possibly shed some light upon his whereabouts, it was decided that he would be made an example of. He was an easy target, and when news of his involvement was leaked to the press, the public were understandably calling for his execution.'

Lady Agnes looked around at the sea of grim faces. No-one spoke. Outside the wind was resting.

It seemed the entire world had stopped to listen to the old lady's tale.

'One day...' she continued, 'a call came in to the boy's parents from the kidnapper, while the stable hand was in the kitchen with the house-keeper. The woman reported this to the police at the time but was 'advised' to stay silent, that she would be suspected as an accomplice if she got involved. I'm sure the family and their staff doubted Mr Turner's guilt. After all, they'd known him as a child. His late father was a much-loved and loyal member of the household staff, and everyone knew that Michael adored the little chap. But the public were baying for blood, and it seemed the police had their man.'

'Incredible!' said Arthur, suddenly jumping up. 'So Travers was right after all. The senior officer suspected Turner's involvement and used unscrupulous means to extract a 'confession,' but his principal aim was to find the child before it was too late. The chief of police however covered this up for his own selfish ends...'

'He'd secured a result and undoubtedly received a pat on the back for a job well done,' scoffed Ellen.

'And Judge Barnes KC sent a poor simple-minded fellow to his death, to protect his friend,' said the professor sadly. 'And he too received a handsome reward and the King's commendation for his pains.'

'And the family of the poor child paid the ransom before Turner was arrested, as I recall,' said Robert.

'Yes,' ventured Travers. 'And his poor mutilated body was found in woodland, three weeks after Turner's execution.'

'Really!' cried out Ellen in horror.

The soldier turned to glare at Travers, his anger and disgust evident.

'But Lady Agnes, why didn't you do something about it?' Ellen said.

'What could she do, go to the police?' scoffed Travers. 'Besides, what use was this information after the man had hanged? Lady Agnes couldn't have known until then. The law forbids discussing the details of an ongoing case with anyone.'

'I didn't,' sobbed the old lady. 'I didn't know and now not only have I lost my husband, I will have to live with this for the rest of my life.' She cried as if her heart would break, and Ellen stood up to comfort her.

'What we have learned tonight should not leave this room,' said the professor, and the others turned to look at him in disbelief. 'Lady Agnes has suffered enough and as for—for the judge,' he said, unable to bring himself to use his name, 'be sure his own judgement day is at hand. He is beyond our censure.

According to the papers, Turner had no family. There is nothing to be gained from taking this any further.'

'Surely man!' exclaimed Arthur. 'A criminal and morally reprehensible injustice has taken place, I, I...'

'Perhaps the professor is comfortable with turning a blind eye, Mr McLaren,' said Travers with a knowing smile. The professor coloured and looked uncomfortable.

'I appreciate that, Professor,' said Lady Agnes, 'but the stationmaster is right. I make no excuses for my husband, nor do I condone his actions, and I fully intend to make this known. The kidnapper may yet be found. At the very least, I hope to clear poor Mr Turner's name.'

'The *Honourable* Sir Gregory Barnes, KC,' scoffed Robert.

'Let him without sin cast the first stone, Lance Corporal!' said Travers, coolly eyeing the soldier. Robert turned on him angrily.

'And you, Travers, if that be your name at all! How come you have so much inside knowledge about the case?' All eyes turned to the man suspiciously. 'The only way you could know such things is if you were directly involved, say a member of the force... *or the kidnapper!*'

Lady Agnes gasped and the three men tensed as if ready to strike. If Travers was intimidated, he didn't show it.

'Quite a temper you have there, Lance Corporal.' He smirked at the soldier. 'But I'm sorry to disappoint you. You see, I couldn't have committed the evil deed. Rather like your good self, sir, I was in India when the Haughton boy was kidnapped, returning briefly for the trial.'

Lady Agnes suddenly felt unburdened. She refused to feel guilty about this. She refused to feel guilty about anything anymore. After all, she'd done nothing wrong and would do everything in her power to right Gregory's wrongs. In the wake of the hanging, her husband had hidden his culpability well. The way he casually spoke of the case, it was as though he'd talked himself into believing Turner's guilt. Maybe that was the only way he could live with himself.

At that moment, she realised that she didn't love Gregory anymore. If she had been guilty of anything, then she had served her sentence, and with Gregory's death came release. She didn't care if the others judged her. She didn't care what anyone thought. After years of living with a domineering, tyrannical man, she was finally free.

Ellen was still in shock. She would never have suspected the judge of such a foul deed. People's souls were indeed a deep well of dark secrets. An image of George's wife suddenly crept into her mind, and she quickly swept it aside. She looked towards the darkened chimney corner and then looked away. She didn't care to dwell too long on thoughts of Travers and how he knew the things he knew.

Professor Rose just wanted to be home. He was unsettled by recent revelations. He was unsettled by the storm and being stranded in an isolated location. But most of all, he had been unsettled by Travers. Sinister, cool, all-knowing Travers. Why, it was almost as if he could read people's minds. And everyone had something to hide, didn't they?

Arthur's mind was somewhere else entirely. Could he risk walking up the track to the signal-box to find out if young Jack had any more news? How would Meg, his poor old dog, be faring alone in the house with the storm tearing around? Again, why did this have to happen in *his* station? And how long did it take to clear a tree, anyway?

Robert was quietly seething. He was certain he and Arthur had spoken of his time in India while searching the station for the prowler, and Travers was out of earshot. One thing was for sure, though, however Travers knew, it was information in dangerous hands. What manner of creature *was* Travers anyway? How *did* he know so much? Robert wished for ten minutes alone with the man. He would thrash the information out of him. He nibbled nervously at his fingernails, while in the shadowy corner, a silent figure watched.

And what Travers was thinking was anyone's guess.

Seated at his desk, he could see the comings and goings of the entire banking hall. Nervous Norman, the assistant manager Mr Sykes, and Sir Henry Mullen, the bank manager, had been in covert meetings all morning. He'd had an uneasy feeling in the pit of his stomach all day but with a rehearsal later that evening, had put it down to pre-wedding jitters. Now he wasn't sure. Why so cloak and dagger? He was convinced he'd seen Norman giving him funny looks earlier, and Mr Sykes had actually said good morning to him for the first time in eight years, and that was really unusual!

Now with his bank account richer by a whole seventy-five pounds and thirteen shillings, he was more than usually anxious. The cashiers were nervous too, whispering and speculating about the comings and goings of senior staff, but he very much doubted they had done anything they'd need to be worrying about.

Around three as they were preparing to close, Mr Sykes proclaimed there was to be an announcement made and could they all stay behind for five minutes.

There were one or two groans from younger staff members who just wanted to be away after work, but a stern look from the assistant bank manager soon silenced them.

Preparing his end-of-day accounts, he gave a sigh of relief. So they weren't on to him after all! They'd never make a declaration over such matters. Now he was certain the rumours were true and that the announcement was to affirm the impending retirement of Ernest Sykes and the promotion of Nervous Norman. His belief was soon replaced by surprise however, when it was Sir Henry's unexpected and early retirement that was announced, along with the appointment of Sykes as the new bank manager and Norman as his assistant.

Although he hadn't yet been approached, it was evident that with the opening left by Norman's promotion, his future was looking very rosy indeed.

Chapter Twenty-One

The rain was letting up a bit, but the wind had returned with a vengeance. All of the station's windows rattled in their boxes as it ripped across the moor, emitting a strange howling noise. Away from the platforms, it was pitch-black now the lightning had abated, and the thunder still rumbled menacingly in the distance.

Lady Agnes was asleep on a bench in the far corner of the room, giving off gentle snores and seemingly peaceful. Robert was quietly pacing so as not to disturb the old lady, and Ellen watched him, appreciative of his straight back and broad shoulders. Arthur was fetching coal, and the professor stood by the window watching the shadows play chase on the dimly lit platform.

'Strange kind of storm this,' he said to no-one in particular. 'I'm sure I've seen nothing like it.'

Travers remained silent in his corner, his face in shadow.

Ellen got up and began to fiddle with the wireless, finding a foreign station that was playing Ella Fitzgerald. She moved to the chair closest to the fire and watched the flames dance up the chimney back. She found herself feeling sleepy, closing her eyes for a moment, and she felt once more the icy cold fingers probing inside of her mind. She knew instantly that this was Travers. Again she felt violated, like her most intimate feelings were being exposed, like this vile man was controlling her, pillaging her thoughts and toying with her emotions. Suddenly she snapped back to the here and now and walked quickly over to where the professor was stood. Robert too had stopped pacing and came over to join them by the window.

All at once over the heath, each thought they heard a train's whistle. A lingering, mournful sound in the dead of night. They all stared at one another incredulously and strained to listen. Surely it was only the wind, crying out across the vast, empty landscape. Then it came again from out on the wild moor, steaming through the night. The unmistakable sound of an approaching train.

Arthur heard the noise from the coal store and came running in. Lady Agnes stirred in her sleep but did not awaken. Travers came forward from the shadows but did not stand with the others.

'It's a train,' said Ellen. 'Surely!'

'It's a train all right,' replied Arthur, making for the door. 'But something's wrong.'

Ellen stared at the stationmaster, a feeling of dread rising in her stomach.

'What do you mean, something's wrong?' cried the professor. 'They're running trains again. We can all go home.'

'You'll find no passenger train at this God-forsaken hour,' said Travers.

'Listen,' said Robert. 'Arthur's right. Something is terribly wrong.'

They listened as the sounds got closer. Soon enough even the clunking of the side irons was discernible.

'Arthur,' said Robert, 'how close is the nearest line approaching us from the west?'

'There *is* no line approaching us from the west. The nearest east-west bearing line is over twenty miles away at Shearing's Vale.'

'It's just the sound carrying in the wind,' said Ellen. 'It's deceptive.'

Robert and the others followed Arthur onto the platform. Travers hovered in the doorway. Lady Agnes slept on.

'The wind is blowing off the sea, dear, from the east,' the professor told Ellen. 'It couldn't be carrying a sound from the north, south, *or west* towards us.'

'Of course,' she replied, a little testily. 'I'm tired is all.'

'But there are no visible signal lights from the north or south,' said Arthur. 'That train is very close,' he looked at the two men with concern, 'and is coming towards us at great speed, from the west, over non-existent tracks.'

'Oh no!' said Ellen backing into the doorway, her fear rising. 'It's not possible! No, no.'

'Even in the howling wind, the train was loud enough to be heard,' said Arthur. 'Which in itself is strange.' He suddenly looked old and weary. As if the events of the evening had abruptly caught up with him. 'It must be almost upon us, and in all my years on the railway, and without having to look at any schedule, I have never had a train run through my station that I haven't been aware of long before its arrival.'

The soldier looked puzzled. 'What do you mean, Arthur?'

'What I mean is, you can sense that a train is coming long before you see or even hear it. You can smell it if the wind is in the right direction, but the tracks will warn of a train's approach a good while before the signal comes in. They'll hum. You can feel a vibration deep beneath your feet. The whole atmosphere becomes charged with it.'

'But it is charged!' cried the professor looking about him. 'Can't you feel it?'

The air *was* charged, with menace! It was as if an electrical current ran between those standing on the platform, infecting each man with fear. The atmosphere was alive, and it was nothing to do with the storm. The three men stood frozen, and Ellen was petrified as the phantom train hurtled invisibly towards them. Then all at once they saw it, shrouded in mist, the glow of the furnace on the footplate like the beam of a warship's search light, slicing through fog. The train thundered past, and inexplicably, contradictory to what they believed they had heard, it was travelling north along the track. But there was no-one on the footplate, and likewise in the four well-lit carriages it drew.

The rush of air as it sped through almost knocked the three men back, but Ellen and Travers were safe in the doorway of the waiting room. The smell of burning coal now filled the air, and the train appeared for all intents and purposes as real to them as the station building itself. But as they watched it disappear into the distance, they saw with horror that the train wasn't running on the track at all but a good foot above it. They stared, unable to look away until, as quickly as it had appeared, the train simply melted into the night. Not becoming a speck on the horizon as a real train would have done, but vanishing, dispersing into the enveloping darkness.

Ellen swayed unsteadily on her feet, not noticing Travers holding up his arm to support her. The professor wiped rain and perspiration from his face, holding his hankie to his eyes as though he couldn't bear to see any more. Robert's mouth felt dry, the need for a good stiff drink imperative. Arthur stood silently at the very edge of the platform, staring into the distance as though the answer to the mystery of the disappearing train lay there.

Suddenly they heard a sound that froze the very blood in their veins—a sickening, bone crunching thud and then a piercing scream that filled the night. The wailing, torturous scream of a woman, so loud and shrill that it hurt their ears. Robert ran forward to try to find the source, but Arthur grabbed his sleeve.

'The woman,' cried Robert, struggling to be heard against the howling wind, whose ferocity had suddenly increased. 'We have to help her!'

'There is no woman,' called out the professor wearily. 'It's all an illusion.'

'And the train?' the soldier said.

'An illusion,' said the professor, almost inaudibly now. Then taking Ellen's hand, he led her gently back inside. 'All an illusion.'

Robert followed him in and saw the old lady had awoken and was staring at them all with bleary-eyed confusion. He looked at the others and shook his head.

Only Arthur remained outside on the platform, the wind whipping at his face as the rain beat down, soaking his exposed head and running down the back of his collar. He stayed that way for a little while just staring into the night, into the darkness and along the twisting track that led to Clarings Brook and railway bridge three-sixty-one.

Chapter Twenty-Two

'But how can it be possible?' whispered Robert to the professor. Arthur had gone to his office and the ladies were visiting the facilities. 'I mean, we all witnessed it.'

'We're all tired, son,' said the professor kindly, his eyes rheumy, his face looking gaunt in the flickering light of the fire.

'We can't all have imagined it,' Robert cried and then lowered his voice. 'It was real. All of my senses told me so.'

'Mass hysteria,' ventured Travers from the corner. 'Sounds from out on the moor lent suggestion of an approaching train. Our tired minds and overwrought imaginations filled in the blanks.'

'Don't be ridiculous man,' sneered Robert. 'We all saw the same—'

'And how do you know we all saw the same, Lance Corporal?' said Travers, standing and joining them by the fire. Robert looked at the man with disdain.

'I saw but a flashing light and felt an almighty gust of wind rushing by. And you Professor Rose?'

'I, I... I'm not so sure anymore. I could have sworn it was a train, but...'

'Seriously sir!' exclaimed Robert incredulously.

'I don't know,' said the professor. 'I'm so tired and still in shock after the death of Sir Gregory and the revelation, but Travers is right. Mass hysteria is a proven phenomenon. We can't even begin to unravel the complexities of the human mind, Robert.' He sighed wearily.

'And you, Travers,' snarled Robert. 'You seem to be an authority on most things. Who or what are you, man?'

Travers smiled pleasantly. He seemed to enjoy getting a rise out of the soldier.

'You could say I am a parapsychologist, sir. I study and have a keen interest in anomalies, events that occur outside the boundaries of what we would perceive to be the 'norm.' I also have a fascination with the untapped potential of the human mind.'

'You mean you enjoy playing *games* with the mind,' scoffed the soldier. 'Like you did with the judge. How can anyone trust a word you say?'

'Let's not have hostility, gentlemen, please,' sighed the professor. 'We have enough to contend with without this.'

The soldier glared at Travers, his rising anger palpable. The friction between the two men hung over them like a gathering of storm clouds, charged and heavy. Still, the mocking smile never left Travers' lips.

'The professor's right, Lance Corporal. We should make good what little time we have left in each other's company. Perhaps we could discuss our respective experiences of India?'

'Why you—' The soldier lunged at Travers, taking him by the lapels and driving him back against the chimney breast. His eyes were steely, narrow slits, his teeth gritted. He knew he was giving Travers ammunition, but he was fuelled with rage, and he pulled back to swing at the man in front of him.

'Gentlemen, please!' said Lady Agnes sharply. 'Ellen and I will not bear witness to such loutish behaviour.'

The two ladies had returned from the WC and stood by the corridor entrance, glaring at the two men. Robert's hands dropped reluctantly by his side, but he couldn't tear his eyes away from Travers, whose face was lit up in triumph and whose mouth was twisted into a mocking leer. He had never once lost his composure, and Robert felt as though he were being toyed with.

'Come, Robert,' said Ellen, leading him away.

'I'm making tea for everyone, and I'd be grateful if you can help me carry it back.'

Robert and Ellen stood in the station's tiny kitchen. Ellen filled the kettle and prepared the teapot while Robert rinsed out the mugs. There was an uncomfortable silence between the two, Robert still inwardly fuming from his brush with Travers. Ellen tried to make small talk.

'I'll be glad to be home.' She smiled at the soldier. 'My aunt will be beside herself. And you, Robert, have you someone at home waiting for you?'

'My wife and daughter,' he returned noncommittally, not looking up from his task.

'What an unexpected and terrible business,' she replied. 'I'd feel better if we had some way of alerting our families.'

As Robert passed her the mugs, their fingers brushed. It was like a shot of electricity for Ellen, and she flinched. For a moment she looked into his eyes, but his face was expressionless. She felt light-headed all at once and swayed. Robert grabbed her arm anxiously.

'Are you all right, Ellen?' The concern was evident in his voice. The teacher almost fell into him, and for a moment he held onto her shoulders at arms' length, studying her face, before pulling over a seat. She dropped into it gladly.

'I'm fine, honestly,' Ellen cried, embarrassed by the attention. 'I was just feeling a bit giddy. I'm so tired and nervous, what with Sir Gregory and all…'

Robert leant across her in the tiny space to switch off the kettle, which was whistling fit to blow its lid. As he did so, her hair brushed his face, and it smelled like apple. He thought of his wife and was worried, not only for her immediate concern as to his whereabouts, but for their future long term and in the coming weeks.

Then, from the waiting room they heard a commotion. The pair looked at one another apprehensively. Ellen groaned wondering how much more they were meant to endure. Passing the booking office, they saw Arthur frantically looking through the contents of a drawer. He found what he was looking for and held up a set of keys. A puzzled frown marked his face.

'Arthur?'

Arthur jumped when the soldier spoke. He hadn't heard Ellen and Robert come in.

'Didn't you hear it?' he asked the bewildered pair. 'We all heard it! We were sat in the waiting room when we heard someone walking about in the corridor. The professor and myself went through to see who it was and…'

'There was nobody there,' finished Robert.

'No, but the rear door was wide open and banging in the wind. I locked that door myself not ten minutes ago when I went out for coal. I can swear to it. It was dark, and I dropped the keys into the coal bucket and had to fumble around for them.'

'And you're certain the door was locked properly?'

'Absolutely, Miss,' said Arthur, noticing how pale the teacher looked. 'After tonight's little episode with the intruder, I double checked. I'm the only one who has the keys to the station. The spare set is locked away in this drawer… here.' He waved both sets of keys at them.

'Then it's evident,' said the soldier, 'that someone's playing with us. The question is who… and why?'

After a full investigation of the station buildings and their surroundings yielded nothing, six nervous strangers locked themselves into the waiting room and huddled by the fire. Lady Agnes had surprised all by suggesting a game of gin rummy, at which she thrashed Arthur, the professor, and Robert in succession. Robert paced restlessly, complaining about his rumbling stomach, and Travers seemed to be sleeping. It was clear that sleep was the last thing on the minds of the others, and the mugs of tea had been set aside in favour of whiskey and brandy, courtesy of Arthur.

Ellen couldn't stop thinking of her poor Aunt Iris, alone and anxious. She made her way over to the window and watched the angry, rolling clouds. She sighed. It seemed like they'd been in the waiting room forever, yet dawn seemed so far away. She felt nervous, apprehensive, but strangely excited. She knew there was more to come before this night was over.

Outside was calm. The storm had abated but the clouds were heavy and menacing. The wind had caused havoc on the platform, and everywhere was sodden and miserable. It was too dark to see past the opposite platform, though the moon was trying to break through the cloud cover. It suddenly reminded her of a poem.

> *'From the lightning in the sky*
> *As it passed me flying by,*
> *From the thunder and the storm,*
> *And the cloud that took the form*
> *When the rest of Heaven was blue*
> *Of a demon in my view.'*

'What's that, dear?' said Lady Agnes. 'I can't quite hear you. Speak up.'

'Oh!' said Ellen, discomfited. She turned to face them all, hand clutching her throat. She coloured, quite unlike Ellen. She hadn't realised she'd been speaking out loud.

'Sounded like poetry,' said the old lady kindly, noticing the teacher's embarrassment. 'Is it one of yours?'

Ellen mumbled, her throat suddenly parched.

'*Alone*,' said Travers, from out of the shadows, and startling everyone who were certain he was sleeping. 'By Edgar Allen Poe,' he said rising. 'It's one of my favourites. Does it have fond connections for you, Miss Potter?'

He smiled at Ellen, and she slid into the nearest seat and covered her face, certain Travers was about to turn his attention on her, as he had the judge. Lady Agnes walked over to her. Concerned the younger woman might be upset, she sat beside her.

'I'm fine, seriously. I'm fine. It just reminded me of… well it was the clouds, they put me in mind of…'

She sighed, suddenly feeling a need to unburden herself to this kindly lady, who had been recently so open among strangers. She smiled half-heartedly at Lady Agnes.

'Someone I knew, he, he had a quote for every scenario, every situation.'

She looked up wearily at Travers, who had walked over to join them. He smiled and nodded. Again Ellen sighed, resignedly.

'George Sinclair and I worked together at a grammar school in York. I taught English and he was the history master…' Ellen paused. The three other men looked over, unsure of what was about to come, unsure of how it had come about.

'And while George was not a man many would consider handsome,' Ellen continued, 'too thin, too studious and lacking even a modicum of humour, I loved him almost immediately.' She smiled to herself. 'I loved his gentle manner and sad eyes, his

139

strange sense of style and the way he blushed whenever I spoke to him… and I knew despite his being a married man, that he had feelings for me, too.'

'I'm not sure you should be telling us this, Miss.' Robert shifted uncomfortably.

'I think Ellen might feel better for getting things off her chest,' said Lady Agnes. 'I know I do. Of course, it's entirely up to her.'

Ellen shook her head sadly and looked down at her lap. She nervously played with her fingers as she spoke, constantly twisting her gold dress ring as a comforting gesture.

'One particular night, we were both working late in the library. It was getting dark early, and although I lived but a stone's throw from the school, George insisted he see me home safely. I remember it was quite a nippy night, an early frost I believe, and I was ill-prepared for it, having only brought a lightweight jacket. Well George, being a gentleman, lent me his coat. I declined, but he insisted, offering his arm so I wouldn't slip on the frosty pavement.'

She looked up at the expectant faces in the waiting room. Travers nodded as if to move her along.

'I was already besotted, you see?' she said, turning to Lady Agnes. 'Wrong I know, and although

I may not be in the first flushes of youth, I was quite unused to a gentleman's attention.'

She paused and cleared her throat before continuing.

'My sister and I lived close to the university campus and the students had spilled out onto the pavement. One particular group of young men was being quite rowdy, and a couple of them called out to us as we neared. I was feeling ill at ease and urged George to hurry along and to take a different route home to avoid passing them, when he stopped and took my hand and led me down a quiet side street. I could hear the young men whistling and jeering and generally being rather crude, and I looked up into George's beautiful kind eyes and then...'

Ellen felt suddenly tearful. She stopped and covered her face.

'You needn't continue, dear, if it upsets you,' said Lady Agnes, taking Ellen's hand and gently rubbing it like a mother might do to a distressed child. Ellen smiled at her, thankful for the kind gesture.

'George and I started to see quite a bit of one another. It all started out innocently enough. We would meet and take tea at Betty's, which was quite the thing. Sometimes we'd go to the Rialto and afterwards he would walk me home. His wife,

Madeline, was a sickly woman prone to melancholia. They were a childless couple, and I know George was not happy in the marriage. They had been childhood friends, and I believe he married her for that reason only. Their families were friends, and I suspect he was coerced into doing so.'

She glanced across at Robert, but he wouldn't meet her eye. She carried on, a sick feeling rising in the pit of her stomach.

'We loved each other so, we really did. George lamented ever having met his wife, but I knew he would never leave her... unless...'

'Unless...' ventured Travers.

Ellen sighed miserably and mumbled something incoherent.

'Speak up, dear,' said Lady Agnes.

Suddenly Ellen began to sob, trying to speak but unable to stop the flow of tears, her whole body wracked with the violence of it.

'Someone *do* something. Oh please, please stop, dear child,' said Lady Agnes, distraught at the spectacle unfolding. It seemed so unlike the woman. Ellen had seemed strong, independent, and single-minded, and Lady Agnes had found herself liking her very much. She doubted anything the young woman could say would change that. Travers took a step forward, offering his handkerchief to her. He took

Ellen firmly but gently by the shoulders. The soldier leant forward in his chair and watched the pair closely.

'Ellen, you'll feel much better for sharing your burden.'

The teacher looked at up Travers and for the first time saw only kindness and genuine concern in his eyes and in his warm smile.

'Thank you, Mr Travers,' she sniffed, dabbing her eyes. 'I believe you're right.' She cleared her throat. 'When it became clear to me that George wasn't happy in the marriage I... I started to wonder whether it would be better if his wife were to find out that we'd been spending time together.'

Lady Agnes tutted and shook her head.

'I was infatuated with him. Madeline's feelings didn't even come into it.' Her tears had dried now and there was a steely determination to her voice. The others looked at this new Ellen with a mixture of bewilderment and contempt.

'One day she visited him at the school. I happened to be passing through reception at the time and the school secretary asked me if I knew where Mr Sinclair was, as his wife was here and she couldn't get hold of him. I stood frozen to the spot for a moment. Then I turned to look at her, my rival, the wife of the man I loved. She was pretty enough,

143

but so pale, so fragile. I suddenly felt insanely jealous. I know it was amiss, that Madeline was the one wronged in all of this, not me, but I couldn't help myself. I told the secretary that I believed he was in the library and that she should find one of the pupils and have them take Mrs Sinclair up. That I felt sure he wouldn't mind. I knew George had been marking the students' work and was alone, so I hurried on up there. I wanted her to see us. Wanted things brought to a head. I was certain she would leave George. Ahead of that I couldn't see. I was blinded. A fool.'

She paused.

Around the room silence lay heavily. Robert, arms outstretched, head to the floor, began rocking in his seat. The flimsy chair creaked in protestation. Arthur was rubbing his sore knee. The professor looked uncomfortable. Ellen looked over at the fire, its amber glow reflecting the unshed tears in her soft green eyes.

She took a deep breath. 'Sure enough, Mrs Sinclair was brought up to the library as suggested and according to plan walked in and caught George and I embracing. We would never normally do so on school property, but to my shame, I pretended to be upset over something, and so George comforted me. His wife let out a blood-curdling scream and ran as fast as she could from the building. George was

144

horrified and gave me a look that made my blood run cold and then ran after her...

'The secretary, unable to find a free pupil, had escorted Mrs Sinclair herself and had witnessed the whole sorry affair,' continued Ellen. 'I had no option but to confess to having engineered the whole thing, claiming that George, unaware of my feelings toward him, was merely offering comfort. Naturally I was suspended indefinitely. George, who took leave until the end of term, never contacted me again.

'For weeks I never left the house. My family were mortified and naturally my job was at stake. The worst thing was, I began to wonder if I had ever really loved George at all... Soon it became imperative I leave York. The school offered to give me a glowing reference with regards to my work if I offered to, *move on*, I believe was the term used. But there were no immediate openings to be found. I became desperate, and then the unthinkable happened...'

Outside, a fresh spate of rain hurled itself at the windows. From somewhere distant, a low rumble of thunder growled. It seemed like a wild beast whose fury all spent, was keen to let its adversary know that the threat of danger was still present. Ellen wrung her hands, rolling and twisting Travers' handkerchief in her tightly clenched fists.

'Madeline, it seems, never recovered from the shock of what she had seen in the library. Her nerves were shot. She became even more withdrawn and was confined to her room. She refused to speak to anyone, especially George, whom I believe she never spoke to again however much he begged and pleaded. One afternoon, George had to take a trip into town, and he promised Madeline he wouldn't be too long. The trip must have taken him longer than he anticipated and when he returned…' She gave a deep sigh, her sorrow plain to see. A teardrop traced its way down her cheek, others set to follow. 'When he returned, he found Madeline slumped across the bed, her face and lips blue.'

'Oh!' cried out Lady Agnes.

'No, she wasn't dead,' said Ellen dully. 'No, she'd taken every pill she could lay her hands on. So the newspapers said, and if George had found her one minute later... Well. They rushed her to hospital, and when she finally awoke, she was… how shall I say it? A vegetable? Brain damaged beyond repair.'

Ellen paused.

'Lack of oxygen to the brain!' said the professor. 'Poor girl. What a terrible business.'

'I'm sorry, Madeline,' Ellen whispered, the tears now streaming down her face. Not sobs. Silent, heartfelt tears. Tears of genuine remorse. She hugged her arms to her chest. 'So, so sorry... I didn't mean...'

'Yes... terrible. A terrible burden,' cried Lady Agnes.

Ellen sniffed and wiped the tears from her cheeks. Her eyes were red and puffy, and she suddenly looked much older.

'It's hard to believe that terrible incident was only a few weeks ago. The newspaper reported the attempted suicide. Gossip spread, despite the school's vain attempts at keeping the affair under wraps. The people in town shunned my family. They threw things at the windows and shouted horrible things as they passed. George, it seems, suffered none of the backlash. He was considered to have suffered enough, and so he had, poor fellow, so he had.'

'Then, I received a letter from my aunt in Redcar. She had managed to secure me a position in a school in Northumberland in which she had been headmistress. She is the one I am going to visit. Or I was before this dreadful storm.'

After a moment's silence, Ellen blew her nose and composed herself. 'I hope you will never have cause to feel the remorse I'm feeling right now. In the grips of a terrible infatuation, I robbed that woman of her marriage and then her life. I can only pray that the Lord will forgive me this terrible indiscretion.'

No one had any words of comfort for Ellen. No words seemed appropriate. Travers returned to his corner.

'I will take these feelings of remorse to my grave,' the teacher said softly to no-one in particular. 'And I will forever be haunted by images of Madeline as she was on that day we first met in the school reception hall.'

'Your admission of guilt was indeed brave,' said Travers. Just a voice. A silhouette in a darkened corner. 'Guilt and remorse are temporary bedfellows, and I'm sure time and opportunity for atonement will be plentiful.'

The weary travellers sat in subdued silence. The station at Little Hubery stood frozen in time, like a relic from the past. Not even the wind could be heard, nor the ticking of the clock in the old waiting room.

Across the room, Robert seemed agitated. The professor looked suddenly sad and dejected. Ellen felt somehow cleansed. A subdued Lady Agnes was thinking how she would never have guessed Ellen could harbour such a dark secret.

In his shadowy nook, Travers' smile never once waivered.

In a small storeroom at the back of the station, a body lay shrouded in a blanket. Nearby, a shadowy figure stood outside the kitchen window, his face a pale mask in the dimly lit surrounds. A thin hand felt around the window frame for a niche and found one. The man slid open the sash and climbed in…

Ellen had fallen asleep, exhausted by her ordeal. The others, shocked by the revelation, sat in brooding silence. Robert's agitation increased. He had drunk a little more than he should have on an empty stomach. Travers was troubling him, although he now seemed more devil's advocate than demon. It still begged the question, how the hell did he know so much about the others, complete strangers stranded in the waiting room? Waiting room? What were they waiting for anyway in this eerie place with the telephone lines down and people creeping around the station? Surely now the storm had abated, he and Arthur could walk into town. He approached the stationmaster, who shook his head doubtfully.

'We're a small backwater, I'm afraid. Even if we could make it across the sodden moorland, which in itself is extremely doubtful, we'd never be able to get a car back to the others. The roads will be flooded for miles around and who knows what damage the wind has done. The lines are down. I can't even see the signal lights anymore. I've lost contact with the box. Far better we stay within the safe confines of the station than go wandering about before daybreak.'

'Safe confines, huh?' Robert felt as if the station walls were closing in on him. Never before had he felt so helpless, like a small creature, trapped, unable to free himself from the constraints of the waiting room, but Robert thought back to his time spent alone trying to cross the moor and the horrors that had awaited him there. He let out a small laugh bordering on hysterical. Perhaps Arthur was right. Despite events in the station, the moor was the more dangerous of the two.

He slumped into the nearest chair. His weariness was evident, but his nerves kept him on edge.

'Why don't you try to get some sleep. We'll—'

Arthur stopped dead at the look of horror on the soldier's face. Suddenly he heard a cry of fear from Lady Agnes and turned to look behind. Everyone in the room except the sleeping Ellen sprang to their feet and were staring with fear and shock towards the dark corner and the door that led into the corridor and back rooms of the station.

Chapter Twenty-Four

The soldier crept forward and signalled to the stationmaster to stand tight against the wall to the right-hand side of the door. The others watched in horror as the door slowly opened, revealing the darkness beyond. The professor put a protective arm around the old lady, who sat mouth agape, paralysed with fear.

Everyone held their breath. Travers crept forward from his corner by the fire and watched expressionless as a form materialised slowly from the shadowy corridor. Robert quick as a flash raised his arms and dealt the emerging figure a blow to the shoulder blades that sent him crashing to the floor.

'That's him!' screamed the old lady. 'That's the ghost.'

'Percy?' Arthur cried in astonishment to his recumbent clerk as the man lay moaning on the floor. 'What the bloody hell are you doing creeping round the station at night?'

Arthur and Robert helped Percy to his feet and he winced, looking warily at the soldier who had dealt him the blow.

Ellen, disturbed by the fracas, sat up, rubbing her hazy eyes, and stared bemused at the stranger before her.

'Well, Percy?' said Arthur, as confused as the rest.

Ernest Sykes didn't like him at all, of that he was certain! And the newly appointed manager of the bank ruled with an iron fist. But with an exemplary work record, the soon to be son-in-law of Mayor Sir William Bainbridge knew he was first in line for promotion to Nervous Norman's old position of supervisor. In two weeks' time, he would be married. He'd bought his fiancée the ring she desired and booked their honeymoon to Venice.

He'd kept a record of monies he had taken from each account and fully intended, on his promotion to supervisor, to pay them back. Gradually of course, plus a little added interest to cover what they would have earned. He wasn't a bad man, not really. It wasn't really fraud, was it? Just a loan to tide him over. He'd make good on his promotion. Then he could settle down to married life and his new job at the bank. God willing.

Chapter Twenty-Five

They led Percy to a chair by the fire, and Arthur poured him a brandy. His clothes were wet, and he shivered uncontrollably as he gazed into the flames, sheepishly glancing from time to time at the pacing soldier, who glared back with undisguised hostility.

'Percy?' repeated Arthur, unable to hide the irritation in his voice.

'I've been sleeping at the station, Arthur,' Percy said flatly. 'Dorothy and me, we've been having a few problems.' He looked around, embarrassed at having to disclose his personal business to strangers, the others equally embarrassed at having to bear witness to it.

'You idiot,' chided Arthur. 'You know it's against railway company regulations. You could have come and stayed at the house.'

'I'm sorry, Arthur. I didn't think. I felt I had nowhere else to go.' Percy stared morosely at the fire, and Arthur wondered how he'd not noticed the change in his normally cheerful clerk. He tapped him on the back.

'Try not to worry, Percy. We'll deal with this later.'

'We thought you were a ghost, Percy,' said Lady Agnes, smiling at the shivering clerk. 'That clears up that mystery, at least.'

'It doesn't explain everything that's happened though, does it?' replied Ellen. 'I mean, it explains our intruder, but what about the other things?'

'Other things?' Percy looked up at Arthur, puzzled.

'Radio interference, phone lines down, that kind of thing. What with the storm and the untimely death of our friend, things have been really creepy down here tonight.'

Percy shuddered. 'I saw the, the… I knew you were still in the station. I fully intended to try to weather the storm, but it proved too much. I thought of lying low in the back room until morning, but then I saw… who?' he said, looking around. Then he realised one of the older gentlemen was missing. 'What happened?'

'Maybe you scared him to death, you bloody fool!' Robert retorted angrily. 'What the hell were you thinking?'

Percy winced and hung his head. 'I'm sorry to frighten you all. I didn't know what else to do.'

'That's enough, Robert,' Ellen said curtly. 'Can't you see the poor man's been through enough?'

'Judging by the bluish tinge around his lips,' the professor interjected in response to Percy's unanswered question, 'we think Sir Gregory had a heart attack.' He smiled tenderly at Lady Agnes. 'It could have happened at any time.'

'And what about the ghost train?' said Ellen, addressing the stationmaster. 'You saw it.'

'I saw something, I confess,' said Arthur, made uncomfortable by the scrutiny. 'But my dear, we're all exhausted and under a great deal of stress. We have just witnessed the death of a gentleman and it's not every day one sees a dead body!'

He looked over at Lady Agnes. 'I'm sorry.' He offered her his heartfelt apologies, as though he'd forgotten she was present.

'I've seen plenty,' said the soldier grimly.

'I've seen more than I could ever want to,' replied the professor sadly.

All eyes turned to him.

Chapter Twenty-Six

'My old school friend, Francis, and I were the best of pals since infancy,' Professor Rose began. 'Our parents were friends, and we were inseparable for a good many years. Francis was very small for his age, and he was a quiet, gentle boy, but I have never in all my days of academia known such intellect, such brilliance, nor anyone with such an extraordinary capacity for learning and storing information.'

He smiled to himself, a sad smile of memories faded with time, of innocence lost. The others waited patiently.

'The boy was an undisputed genius and although I strived hard to keep up, I'm afraid I paled in comparison. Truth is, I would not have achieved what I have academically were it not for his support and his persistence. But my story, I'm afraid, is an old one.'

A loud clap of thunder overhead made Ellen jump. She looked earnestly at the professor.

'As we grew older, so we grew apart. Not that we weren't still friends, but I got in with a rather rowdy crowd and Francis, hard as he tried, was simply not accepted.' He looked around at the faces of his companions. 'He was introverted you see, not very physical, and the other fellows mocked him. In fact, they bullied him over his lack of prowess on the sports field and for his gentle nature, and to my shame, in my desperate need to belong, I also belittled and ridiculed my dearest friend.' He sighed. 'Now don't take me wrong, I was no Stanley Engelhart, but I was a mean bowler and wicket-keeper, and I could hold my own at football, too.'

Arthur broke away from the gathering to make Percy and the others a hot drink and tend to the fire.

'One evening, we were all celebrating the end of our exams and had managed, with the help of one of the older boys, to smuggle two bottles of cheap scotch into our dormitories.' He paused. 'Not being used to such strong liquor, or any liquor at all for that matter, we soon lost control. Francis, who in an aim to prove himself had drunk the most, had become bolder by the minute.' The professor shook his head as the memories came flooding back. 'Suddenly Wareing, one of the head boys, stood, and we all followed him outside to the bell tower where the school flag hung. I was terrified. I knew what he would do. He dared Francis to climb the tower and steal the flag. I begged him not to do it, but he pulled away from me and with an amazing fleetness of foot, scaled the ivy-clad trellis on the side of the tower.'

The professor sat wringing his hands. Arthur returned with hot drinks and settled by the fire with the others.

'The lads cheered him on, but I couldn't look. I knew he was trying to impress me and my friends, to prove himself worthy of being one of the boys. I also knew I was partly to blame. He soon reached the parapet and climbed over, and with a sigh of relief, I waved to him at the top.'

'Thank you,' said the professor with a smile, taking a steaming mug from Arthur. He took a sip, and the hot liquid singed his lips. He continued.

'He removed the flag as we watched intently, the boys spurring him on, but for reasons known only to himself, he removed the pole, too, instead of just unclipping the flag. We shouted up to him *no*, Francis, *no*, but he seemed not to hear us. He was just under half-way down when the edge of the flagpole he was carrying under his arm got caught in the trellis. He pulled and twisted but he couldn't get it loose. *No Francis, leave it*, I cried out. The other boys were silent now, sobered, anxiously watching as the foolish boy tried to remove the pole from the trellis that held it entangled.

'Suddenly the pole broke free. Francis lost his grip on it, the impetus unbalancing him. He tried to cling onto the trellis desperately, crying out in fear for us to save him. I ran forward, but Wareing held me back. *No, you fool, it won't hold the both of you.* I struggled but I knew he was right. I called out my friend's name in horror.'

The others drew in closer. Outside, the wind began to howl. Reflections of dancing flames licked the ceiling.

'All at once, ivy and trellis were pulled away from the wall with the weight of the clinging boy. We all gasped in horror, and it seemed as if, just for the briefest spell, time had stood still. Then everything moved, but really slowly as though time was trying to catch up with itself. A strange expression crossed Francis' face, and he began to plummet towards the ground. For some reason he turned in mid-air before falling. The flagpole had already begun its descent and stuck into the grass at the foot of the tower. And then the unthinkable happened. Francis fell face down with incredible force and impaled himself upon the pole sticking upright in the wet grass.'

The professor sniffed away a tear, embarrassed by his public display of emotion so long after the fact.

'He never made a noise as he fell but let out a grunt as his body was skewered by the pole. For a second or two we stood rigid with shock, and then we all ran forward towards the now-still body of our friend. Wareing retched and then vomited at the sight that greeted us, for the weight of Francis' body had caused it to slide full length down the pole, only its tip pinning him to the ground. *Help me*, I cried as I tried to free him. I knew he was dead, of course I did, but I couldn't bear to see him like that.'

Lady Agnes began to sob, and Ellen put a comforting arm around her shoulders. Percy looked as if he, too, was about to vomit.

'A couple of the boys ran up, adrenalin playing its part as we removed the pole from Francis' back. We turned him around, and although a trickle of blood escaped from his lips, he looked every bit as peaceful as if he were lying out on the lawns in the sun. His eyes were wide as if in wonder, and he smiled peacefully up at us. The boys backed off as if repulsed, and closing his lids with my fingers, I rested my head against his blood-soaked shirt and howled in anguish.'

When he was finished, the professor hung his head in shame and remorse. 'I could have prevented it,' he said sadly. 'He did it to impress me.' Travers placed a comforting hand on one shoulder and smiled at the professor.

'Professor, you were not to blame. It was a boyish prank gone wrong. You couldn't possibly have prevented it. It was just one of those things.'

Everyone looked at Travers in shock. What the hell was this man about? Cruelly probing one minute, offering solace the next.

The wind groaned like a wounded beast and the gaslights flickered and then went out, only the fire illuminating the scene, casting grotesque shadows on the walls. But none were more so than the silhouette of the stooped man who loomed over the broken figure of the professor.

Chapter Twenty-Seven

Arthur watched weary-eyed as the minute hand moved slowly around the clock face. It was a little after four a.m. and the others were sleeping, but exhausted as he was, he could not manage to drop off. Percy and Robert had spread out on the floor in front of the fire, and both ladies were curled up on benches. The professor slumbered where he sat. Even Travers appeared to have worn himself out.

He thought of Percy sleeping at the station. How could he not have known? He smiled on hearing his clerk, snoring peacefully by the fire. Percy wasn't a bad lad, and he was sure all would be fine soon enough between him and his good lady.

The wireless had been switched off and all was silent but for the ticking of the clock. The thunder and lightning had passed over, but the wind still howled around the station building, not with the same ferocity, but enough to drive the pouring rain hard against the waiting room windows.

'What a bloody night,' he thought to himself, looking round at the stranded passengers sleeping as peacefully as babes. Who would have thought when they first settled together by the fire that each one had something to hide? The late judge in the back room, an honourable and respected gentleman, guilty of sending an innocent man to his death. The professor plagued with a deep-seated sense of guilt over a tragic and unfortunate accident. And what of the young lady, Ellen, inadvertently ruining the life of another after falling for her husband! He never could have guessed what colourful characters sat huddled around his waiting room fire. What other secrets would be revealed before the night was out, and what part would the enigmatic Travers have to play in prompting that? Although he knew he himself had led a good, honest life and had no secrets to hide or nothing to fear from Travers, he still felt uneasy in the other man's company. It seemed Travers had been doing his level best to antagonise the soldier, but to what end?

He hoped for no more revelations, no more bombshells dropped. There had been enough horror stories around the campfire this night.

He felt cramped and achy and stretched out his arms and legs, the damaged knee causing a sharp pain to shoot up his thigh. He thought it would be best to try and keep it flexible so it wouldn't seize up, and to this end he decided to walk through and try the phone again, although in truth he held out little hope. Sometimes they were down for several hours, and it was a good job the signal boxes didn't have to rely on them. He thought of radioing down to his signalman. He'd tried a couple of times earlier but was met with the same static that had interfered with the wireless. He knew young Jack wouldn't have much to tell him, isolated as he was in his signal box, but Arthur knew he should keep trying if only to see how the lad was.

When he approached the door to his office, he felt apprehension, like a knot in his stomach. Not fear exactly, but something akin to it. He paused, wondering what was waiting for him behind the door. He knew he had to face whatever it was, but he also knew instinctively that it meant him no harm.

As he entered, the room felt cold; there was also a strange smell, pipe smoke mixed with... he couldn't quite place it, but it was a familiar smell in many ways and one that stirred up long-dormant memories of childhood.

He made his way over to the radio and tried calling out, but the terrible static told him he'd have no joy with the instrument. He turned and was just about to try the telephone again when a figure sat in his chair surprised him, and he let out a startled cry.

'D-dad?' he gasped. His father's shade wavered and fluctuated, now translucent, now solid. The very air around him seemed to quiver as though he had upset the natural balance of things by appearing now to his son. His clothes were colourless and grey as though washed many, many times, and his eyes seemed somehow hollow, lacking soul.

Suddenly, Arthur felt the room spinning. He felt light-headed and had to lean against the wall to stop himself from falling. A mist descended and when his vision cleared, he found himself not in his own office, but in the same room as it had been when it was his father's office all those years ago. Where his father had been sat only a moment ago, the chair was now empty. His old miners lamp stood on the desk beside the Marconi, and his favourite fountain pen and blotter shared a space with an inkpot and some rolled-up sheets. The pigeonholes behind his desk were overflowing with documents, and his barometer held pride of place on the wall. The old clock was the same, but for a few moments it appeared to be going backwards, and then it stopped.

Arthur caught sight of an old picture of his mother and himself when he was but a boy. He was wrapped in a towel, and she was rubbing him and hugging him at the same time. He gave out a small cry.

'I remember when this was taken,' he thought aloud. 'I was seven and we went to Whitby. My dad had just been teaching me to fly a kite on the beach, and I chased it into the sea and got soaked.' He felt tears welling up in his eyes, and then his father walked in.

From beyond the open door, Arthur heard a voice call out, 'Cup of tea, Albert?' It was Walter, Dad's former clerk. Albert and Walter alive again, in the flesh.

Arthur rushed over to his father, but he seemed not to notice him and brushed straight past and sat down at his desk. Arthur felt hurt by the rebuff and turned to look at his father, who was busy with the wireless. He left the office and walked through the booking hall to the waiting room. He could hear Walter in the tiny back room that served as the station's kitchen, whistling 'Underneath the Mellow Moon,' and when he walked through to the waiting room, he gasped in surprise.

The others were gone, and it was daylight, a bright sunny day. The waiting room was full of passengers wearing the clothes of days gone by. Suddenly, a lady wearing a cloche hat and dressed in a jersey blouse and a velour skirt walked straight through him as though he wasn't there. He saw her shudder and felt a jolt of electricity through his entire body. For a second there, they had almost become one. He could feel what she was feeling, could read her thoughts. She was meeting her fiancé and they

169

were to look at rings. She was excited, full of joy and expectation, this lady... Elizabeth. Her name was Elizabeth. The lady turned and he smiled at her, but she seemed to look straight through him.

A voice behind him made him jump. It was Travers.

'They cannot see us, Arthur,' he said, smiling warmly at the stationmaster. 'We're just ghosts in their time.'

'Travers? What is this? Where are we?'

'Why, Arthur,' Travers teased, not unkindly. 'Little Hubery. Do you not recognise your own station?'

'Scarcely,' said Arthur. 'But how? And where are my passengers? I left them sleeping.'

'They're still there.' Travers smiled. 'They have not moved.'

Arthur looked at Travers as if he'd gone mad. Could he see something Arthur couldn't?

'They're where you left them, Arthur, in nineteen thirty-six. This is nineteen twenty-five.' He gestured with a sweep of his arm at the room around him. Arthur looked at him with open-mouthed astonishment.

'It's a time-slip, Arthur. A rare phenomenon, indeed. You are very lucky to have witnessed this.'

'But how, Travers? And why only you and me? Why not the others?'

Travers sighed. 'The others are sleeping. Only you and I were awake when the phenomenon occurred, so only you and I must witness it.'

Arthur looked around him and reached out to touch the wall. It was solid, it was real. He suddenly became suspicious of Travers and wondered what game he was playing now.

'What is this, Travers? How do you know these things? What are you doing here, and why was that lady able to shift through me when the walls feel so solid?'

Travers sighed again, growing impatient. 'The walls *are* solid, Arthur. The station hasn't changed. It's still all around us. Only the timeframe has changed. We are visitors in another time. We are inconsequential. We have no solid form, we're just voyeurs. Spectators in an era past.'

'So none of this is real?' said Arthur.

'Of course it's real, man. It's a real as you or I.'

Suddenly Arthur began to feel anxious, to feel wrong, displaced. He noticed that the lighting had changed and that the people around him seemed to be wavering, solid one minute, ethereal the next. He looked back at Travers and although he could see the other man's lips moving, he couldn't really work out

171

what he was trying to say. His words were slurred and seemed muffled, as though he was in another room. Arthur's unease grew as his surroundings became flat and everything turned still around him. Not even the air moved.

'Travers!' he tried to say but found himself unable to form the word. Arthur turned and walked back through the ticket office. He found he could no longer hear Walter whistling or his father talking or moving around. Everything was deathly silent.

The ground seemed to shift beneath his feet, and he grabbed the door frame for support. Everything went black for a second, and then he found himself staring at his office door. He reached for the handle and pushed. Within, the room had returned to normal. On his desk he could see the telephone and his typewriter, the small table by the window where the wireless normally stood. The fire burned low in the grate and beside it, in his father's old armchair, sat Travers.

Chapter Twenty-Eight

'My father, Albert, took me on as an apprentice when I was fourteen,' said Arthur, passing a drink to Travers. 'I'd grown up around the railway. Before he took over at Little Hubery, he was stationmaster at Shearing's Vale and Doncaster before that, where I was born in the station house.' He pulled up a chair by the fire and sipped his scotch. He felt the need of a stiff drink after his recent experience.

'I started as a ganger, and then apprentice fireman, but that wasn't for me. Eventually, I developed an interest in becoming a signalman, the position I took at Shearing's Vale before being drafted into the army.'

Half of Travers' face was lit by the glow of the fire, and Arthur couldn't help but notice how smooth his face looked. He hadn't realised Travers was so young. He didn't look a day over twenty-five. Even the evening's events didn't seem to have had an effect on him. No shadows showed beneath his eyes, which were clear and bright. He looked, for all intents and purposes, refreshed, like a man who had just had his full eight hours. Sharp contrast to earlier when he'd looked grey, almost ill-looking. Odd!

Arthur again brushed off the uneasy sensation he had come to feel when Travers was around. He continued.

'When, in nineteen-eighteen, my father was moved to Little Hubery following the sudden and unexpected death of then stationmaster, Len Dewsbury, I stayed on as signalman at the Vale four more years before moving to the box at Hubery. Well, I found after so many years, the isolation of being on signal played with my nerves, so when Dad's clerk, Walter, retired in the autumn of twenty–five, I moved into the office there and began to work closely with Albert, who was training me to step into his position when he retired. He was a hard taskmaster and showed me no favours for being his son, but I knew that stepping into his shoes as stationmaster would be no easy challenge, and I worked all the harder to please him.'

'Only a few months after I'd moved to Hubery, we lost Mum to pneumonia. Dad was never the same after that and his health seriously declined. The company had offered him early retirement with full pension after all his years of service, but he refused. He held on until ill health and the company *forced* his retirement. Finally, late summer of twenty-six, I was made stationmaster at Little Hubery.

'For a while, things ran smoothly. Dad was exhausted and spent many of his waking hours by the sea, claiming the fresh salt air was beneficial to his health. But he was a working man, had been since as far back as he could remember, and he was soon bored with the inertia of his days and back at the station, making his presence felt.'

Arthur drained his glass and fell silent for a moment, staring into the flames. Travers watched him patiently, waiting for him to continue with the story.

'As an old-school stationmaster, Dad was always resistant to change, and when he retired, the railway company decided to introduce more modern equipment and methods of working. But Dad wasn't about to make for an easy transition, and nothing could persuade him that his interference wasn't welcome. I really should have foreseen that he would have problems letting go, especially without Mum to fill his days.

'As the weeks and months passed, he had more or less moved back in at the station, and his reluctance to retire was causing me all manner of problems.' Arthur sighed. 'He would undermine me with the workers and override any decisions I would make with regards to staffing and the running of the station.

'One day, he almost caused an accident when he interfered with the running of the signal box and wouldn't allow for the passing on of a message from Clarings Brook. We shouldn't have let a goods train into our section before the points were switched. Of course, I had to ban him from the station by order of the company. This put further strain on our relationship, and as we also shared a home, things became very difficult between us.

'We spent most of our evenings bickering and arguing. Dad was a shadow of his former self, and it's always hard to watch a beloved parent go that way, but more so when he refused to let go. Nothing I could say would persuade him to go out, to meet his friends and enjoy his retirement years.'

Arthur suddenly became morose, and Travers smiled kindly and prompted him to go on.

'On that particular afternoon, we'd spent most of the previous evening arguing about the suitability of a new signalman the company had hired, and I was tired of it, and if the truth be known, tired of him, too.' He hung his head in shame.

'When I left for work that morning, he had begged me to let him go too, claiming he was feeling unwell and just wanted to sit in the office by the fire. He promised not to interfere, but I was adamant that he stay up at the house, especially if he was, as he

176

claimed, unwell. He had used that line several times before so I would allow him into the office, whereupon he had made a miraculous recovery and taken over the running of the station. Promptly at one, I had left the office and gone up to the house to make Dad a sandwich and found him slumped in his chair, staring sightlessly out of the window at the comings and goings of the station.'

Arthur sighed, his feelings of guilt and remorse apparent.

'If only I'd let him come with me. I didn't believe he was ill. I was angry and resentful, and I didn't get to say goodbye. He'll never know how much I loved him.'

Travers stood and walked towards the door, stopping behind Arthur's chair and placing a reassuring hand on his shoulder.

'Arthur, you have nothing to reproach yourself for. You were as good a son as any man could hope for. Your father has no ill feelings towards you. He loves you and wants you to be happy. He wants you to let these feelings go, Arthur. Leave them be and move on.'

Arthur heard Travers' voice emulating that of his father and echoing around the room, and just for the briefest amount of time, he saw him again, smiling from his chair by the fire. He heard the door click gently behind him, but he didn't look round, didn't move for what seemed like an age. He simply sat in his office chair, staring into the flames as the darkness from the moor crept ever closer to the isolated station and its stranded inhabitants.

The sun beat down mercilessly, the heat intensified by the large picture window at the side of his desk. He ran his finger around the inside of his collar in a desperate bid to loosen it and cool himself down a little. If only he could remove his jacket! But he knew that would be frowned upon by his new manager, Sykes. The clerks and tellers were cool in cotton shirts and ties, but as newly-appointed supervisor, he was expected to set an example. It was fine for the bank manager and assistant bank manager to remove their jackets in the comfort of their own offices, their own *fan-cooled* offices, but he, as banking hall supervisor, was customer-facing, so no such concession was made for him.

He shifted awkwardly in his seat. His flesh, only an hour or so since lightly cologned and fresh, felt prickly and sticky, and his back was drenched with perspiration. His discomfort was further heightened by a fresh attack of nerves at the thought of his impending nuptials only two days from now, and after recent purchases, his almost empty bank account, or rather that of his alias, Basil Morgan-

Jones. He groaned as Mrs Baxter entered the banking hall and made a beeline for his desk.

Chapter Twenty-Nine

Robert wasn't sure what had awakened him so abruptly, and he looked around bleary-eyed for a moment or two before focussing on the chimney corner. Travers was strangely absent, but some movement had caught his eye and he stared disbelievingly at what he saw.

A shadow, nebulous and vague, seemed to cover the wall in the very corner, like a mould, and it seemed to be moving, growing one minute, retreating the next. It was black like an ink stain, impenetrable in parts, and these parts too seemed to be moving, thinning out, breaking apart before forming in other areas. In the more opaque parts of the melee, he could just make out shapes forming.

He looked around to see if any of the others were awake, but they all seemed dead to the world. Arthur, he assumed, was in his office. Robert turned back to the alcove.

The shadow seemed to have spread, to be moving down the wall. He felt his chest tighten. His hands felt clammy, his breathing laboured. He tried to move away from the thing in the corner, but he found himself frozen to the spot. He could hear the gentle snores of the professor. The old lady and the teacher also seemed to be sleeping peacefully, as though in telling their stories to the others, they had somehow unburdened themselves.

A strange groaning sound filled the room and seemed to be getting louder, and still the others never stirred. Robert was unsure whether it was the wind in the chimney breast or whether it came from the abomination in the room. Whatever it was, it was his to witness and his alone, for although he tried to cry out, his fears could not find a voice. His windpipe felt restricted, his mouth dry and his tongue unable to detach itself from his lower jaw.

The swirling, black mass moved away from the corner and onto the chimney breast itself, coming to rest on the wall and hovering above the mantle. Unlike before, the room remained warm, the gaslights unwavering, and the fire burned evenly and brightly. Nothing was untoward in the room but for the moving shadow above the fireplace, from which exuded such feelings of hatred and evil towards Robert that he was sure he would die from terror right where he sat, on the floor in front of the fireplace.

From out of the black mist, a hand formed and reached out towards Robert, and then another, both vaporising before reaching him. The centre of the mass converged, and a shape began to form, a torso, but vague and insubstantial, malformed and without a core.

Robert thought his heart would stop when a head formed above the torso, the features ill-defined and tenuous, but features he recognised, nonetheless. It was the man whose murder he had witnessed and not attempted to prevent. A man who would haunt and plague him for the rest of his life unless justice for his untimely and violent death was seen to be done. The head groaned its injustice and twisted this way and that as if in immense pain. Then it fixed its shadowy, black pits of eyes on its antagonist, and a desolate cry rent the still night air.

The thing on the wall extended a long, snake-like neck and its screaming head lunged towards him. Darkness closed in, enfolding Robert in its warm, protective keep.

Chapter Thirty

'Robert? Robert, wake up.' He felt himself being shaken roughly by the shoulder. 'Robert, wake up. You're having a bad dream.'

Robert opened his eyes wide and looked around him at the alarmed faces of the other passengers. Travers had a hand on his arm, and Robert pulled away as if it were contagious. He looked towards the shadowy alcove and up at the chimney breast, but there was nothing. The others stared at him as if he were quite mad, their expressions a mixture of bemusement and concern. Arthur came running in from his office, and Travers gestured for him to stand back.

'Are you well, dear fellow?' remarked the professor. 'You were screaming, old man. Gave us quite a fright.' Travers extended his hand to help the soldier up, but Robert knocked it away aggressively.

'Come,' said Travers. 'You'll feel much better when you've unburdened yourself. Why don't you tell us all about it?'

'You!' the soldier screamed, lunging at him. 'You did this you, you monster. What the hell are you that you know the inside of another's mind?'

Arthur, Percy, and the professor rushed Robert, who fought them fiercely. Soon they overpowered him and pinned him back into a chair. The ladies fled and stood by the ticket office counter, upset by the latest disturbance. Travers held his ground.

Eventually Robert calmed down and stared long and hard into the fire. Troubled by his demeanour but not wanting to bother him further, the others turned to move away, but the soldier called them back. He sighed, and for a minute or two his head fell upon his chest. When he raised it again and looked them all in the eye, his look was grave and deadly serious.

'It's true,' he said sadly. 'I too have a tale to tell. I served with the British Army in India for three years in the Eastern Command, based in Lucknow, North East India. I myself was stationed at a camp in Bengal. Our platoon consisted of four sections. Near the camp was a small village, Adra, next to the town of Haora where we would go for supplies.

'Some of the lads had women in the town, but one of our platoon would sneak off to the village instead. He showed no interest in the women in town and we wondered if he was…you know?' He looked up at the ladies, embarrassed. He cleared his throat and carried on. 'He had no wife at home and kept pretty much to himself, out of the way. A queer sort he was.' Robert rubbed his eyes and paused for such a while that Ellen wondered if he would continue. Eventually, he did so.

'A few times we caught him creeping off and wondered where he went and what he was up to, so one night we followed him. It was just getting dark and some of the village children were still playing in the street. He approached them and offered them chocolate. A couple of them ran away, but he stood talking to the others and then led one of them out of the village.

'We tried to follow him, but he seemed to know the area quite well and disappeared into some trees with the child, a girl aged around six. Some of the men waited for him. They wanted to kill him then and there. Many of us had children, daughters, and I could understand their frustration, their rage, but I wanted him punished through official channels. If he was found guilty, he would be court-martialled, anyway. Justice would be served, but we wouldn't have blood on our hands.

'Before we were able to report the matter, men came from the village for help. The girl was missing. Again, we scoured the area but could find no trace of her. Then someone spotted him, Powell was his name, William Powell, with scratches down his face. He ran away with four of our men plus a couple from the village in pursuit.

'I stayed behind to help with the search. Suddenly I heard a gut-wrenching cry of anguish, a heart-rending scream. I hear it even now, as clear as if it were yesterday. The girl's father stepped out from the trees; he had something in his hands, something limp like a bundle of rags. He dropped to his knees and threw his head back and wailed. I was consumed with pity for the man and horror at what had taken place. But my heart was truly broken when the girl's mother appeared. She coolly and silently walked over to her husband, removed a strand of hair from her daughter's eyes and carried her indoors. Just as calmly as if she'd been sleeping and she was putting the child to bed. The girl's neck lolled at an un-natural angle, and it was obvious it had been broken.'

Lady Agnes gasped, and Ellen groaned and clutched her stomach as if made nauseous by the soldier's tale. Percy looked at Robert in horror, but he carried on, regardless. Once he had begun, he felt an urgent need to tell his story, however harrowing.

'Back at camp,' he continued, 'we searched his cabinet in his bunker and found, erm, souvenirs, among them a girl's slipper, a cheap tin bracelet, and some dead flowers. The men were furious. Some cried, either with rage or because they were fathers away from their own children. A search party was set up, the others having lost Powell when he jumped on a passing lorry heading into town.

'We split up into two groups and then we split again within our group. I was partnered with a young subaltern named Harris, and for a while we managed to stay together in the bustling streets of the town. Then suddenly I found myself having to jump out of the path of an approaching rickshaw, and when I turned back to find Harris, he was gone. I wandered the streets for ages looking for members of my platoon. It was baking hot and dusty, and I looked around for somewhere to buy a drink, and then I heard a ruckus in a nearby alleyway.

'Four of the platoon had Powell up against a wall and were repeatedly punching him.

'I stood back and observed. The men hadn't seen me at that point, but Powell had. He pleaded with me to help, but I watched and waited. It was my intention to see him beaten for what he had done; it was all I could do not to join in. I meant to stop it, to let justice take its due course, but I didn't. I just kept thinking of the children playing in the village street. Of the little girl taking chocolate and being led off into the woods and how we'd failed to protect her. Of her limp body, so small, so frail. Of her father's anguish and her mother's silent tears, and I took solace from every punch and every kick that bastard took...

'Sorry!' He looked at the ladies. 'I wanted him to die, slowly, fearful and in pain as he had caused the death of that poor child, so I stood and I watched. Nobody interfered. The people in the street rushed by, too afraid. I stood there as he was slowly beaten to death and all the while he watched me watching.

'Soon enough, he stopped begging for help and just scrutinised me with a kind of dull bemusement as if to say, *they're killing me. They're killing me and you're just going to watch.* Eventually his body went limp, but still his eyes stared, dull and lifeless like a fish on a slab, not bemused anymore, but accusing. Taunting me with what I had witnessed. The men turned when they realised he was dead, and one caught a glimpse of me as they left. A look of understanding passed between us, no words needed.

'The men didn't run, nor did they look back. No-one followed them or tried to challenge them about what had just happened. I too turned away and began walking in the direction I had just come from, and in a while I saw Harris, looking lost among the street traders and the beggars in the baking sun. *Any joy?* he shouted, waving at me. I shook my head and led him away for a much-needed drink before we headed back to camp.

Naturally it wasn't too long before Powell's body was found. Even in that short space of time, the rats and flies had had their fill of him in that dank and dirty alleyway, and it was nothing less than he deserved.'

'Dear Lord,' cried Ellen, raising her hand to her mouth. Burying her face in her hands, Lady Agnes had slumped forward, as if the weight of sharing the horrific tale was too much to bear. Robert remained stoical, as though rendered numb by the whole experience.

'There was an enquiry into his death of course. By this time I had been called back to England, my squadron stationed at Catterick Camp. Back in India the military had been questioning the men about the incident, and one had caved in, apparently unable to live with himself after the deed. Naturally he didn't implicate any other man, but it was well known by those at camp which men had gone to town to look for Powell in the wake of the little girl's death, and the suspects were soon rounded up.

'I was lucky not to be implicated myself. The young subaltern, Harris, testified that we had spilt from the men and not seen them again until we returned to camp. That saved me from suspicion. But having been placed in town, I have been called as a witness and must testify before a board at Catterick. If I tell the truth of what I witnessed, four good men will die.'

'And if you lie, a man's murder will go unpunished,' said the professor.

'And what of it,' said the soldier. 'He deserved to die for what he did to those children.'

'Who are you to say what man should live and who should die?' Travers spoke out. 'The law decrees he be given a fair trial, and if, as you say, the evidence against him was irrefutable, then he would be put to death anyway. It was not for those men or for you to take justice into your own hands.'

The soldier buried his head in his hands and groaned.

'What do I do? What do I do?' he cried. 'And now the spirit of Powell haunts me. Out there on the moor, here in the station, where before he only haunted my dreams.'

'Only you can decide what's right, Robert,' said the old lady kindly.

'There is only one proper course of action,' said the professor. 'It's up to you whether you take it or condone a lawless society and a breakdown of justice. If one of the men has already confessed, I see little option open to you other than to speak the truth and let justice prevail.'

The others moved away from the soldier, who sat staring into the flames for a good while. Ellen went out to make tea and the old lady followed her. The wind continued to howl, and the rain still pounded the windows.

Thin streaks of light broke through the heavy storm clouds, driving back the night, and within the station, silence pressed heavily against the walls. Finally, the soldier stood and looked at the others.

'I have made my decision,' he announced. 'I know what I have to do.'

Until coming face-to-face with the old lady, Mrs Baxter, he had cleverly covered his tracks concerning his fraudulent deception and the transferring of monies into his alias' account. Faced with his client's concern about discrepancies in her account, a client of whom he was equally as fond as she was of him, he had led her into his managers' office and there had broken down and confessed all.

He had been instantly suspended pending a full and thorough investigation. Only the power and influence of his father-in-law to be, as well as a promise to reimburse all, including any interest lost, kept him from arrest.

'I only wanted the best for Elizabeth.' He sobbed as his fiancée's father led him away, too shame-faced to look his colleagues in the eye. His shame and misery intensified as he heard the old lady wail, 'I would have given him the money if he'd only asked.' Outside, the mayor had warned him to leave and never return. He was never to see Elizabeth again or look to communicate with her.

Thoroughly wretched and dejected, he'd walked out of town and made for the cool, dim shelter of the nearby woodland. There he had sobbed non-stop for the best part of an hour. Tears of remorse, of frustration. Of pain in knowing he had lost his beloved Elizabeth. There beneath the canopy of leaves, in the dim shade of a twisted oak.

Finally, he stood and brushed himself down before beginning the ten-minute walk down the beaten path to the railway line and bridge three-sixty-one.

He leant against the parapet and straightened his tie. The view from bridge three-sixty-one allowed him to see for miles around, but the woodland, coastline, and untamed natural beauty of the surrounding moorland held no charm for him. Not today.

It had been another hot day and the sun was setting on the horizon, weaving braids of fiery red across the sky. The man wiped beads of perspiration from his forehead and looked at his pocket-watch. Only another ten minutes to go and then it would all be over.

He thought of his fiancée and how he'd let her down. He hoped that she'd understand and that one day, she'd be able to forgive him…

Chapter Thirty-One

In his office, Arthur had at last made contact with Shearing's Vale, and he learned that the tree had finally been shifted, the line cleared, and the points and signalling equipment repaired. In the waiting room his passengers slept, unaware that their trial was almost over. The trains would start running a little later than usual, but they would soon be able to go home. He looked at the clock above the mantle. It was almost six. The numbers swam before him. His head suddenly felt too heavy for his shoulders, and all at once, slumped across his desk, the stationmaster slept, too.

Travers, deathly still and silent in the chimney corner, rose and stood beside his fellow passengers, watching the sleeping forms in their repose. Soon each would leave the station and go forward with their lives. Some to the same life, others with very different plans, but each man and woman would awaken and leave the station changed by his or her experiences the previous night, and Travers could be certain that change was for the better.

He smiled to himself as he watched Lady Agnes, her mouth twitching at the corners as she slept. He knew her new life without her husband would take some adjusting to, but he also knew that she was finally free, of living in his shadow and of his burden of guilt. From across the waiting room, he saw the shade of Michael Turner. The young man smiled at him and then turned and walked through the door, disappearing into the darkness of the corridor. Travers looked once more at Lady Agnes, who was smiling as she slept, and he knew beyond doubt that her dreams were at last peaceful.

He sat beside the lovely Ellen, asleep on a bench. Her dreams too were of a rosy future now she had finally admitted to her part in the destruction of Madeline Sinclair's mind. Admitted and more importantly regretted and felt genuine pain and remorse for causing damage to her rival in love. Across the miles, Madeline Sinclair also slept peacefully. She no longer hurt, or even remembered her husband's indiscretion. The feelings of hatred and vengeance had only been a result of Ellen's repressed guilt. Ellen would always feel sorry for the pain she had caused George's wife and the damage their affair resulted in. Her feelings had intensified when she realised that she had never really been in love at all but was in the grips of a terrible infatuation. But she now knew that she had to get on with her life, a good, honest, decent life, where recompense would be paid by kind deeds and thoughtful gestures.

From where he sat, Travers could hear the soldier mumbling in his sleep, but he wasn't in the grip of some disturbing nightmare. He was conversing with the man he had wronged and allowed to die, William Powell. Robert was begging forgiveness from the murdered man and vowing to bear witness at the enquiry and see justice done. Travers knew he was salving his conscience and that the trial and prosecution of the murderers would see an end to his nightmares and peace return to the soldier's life at last.

Also in the land of dreams, the professor played cowboys and Indians with Francis, his childhood friend. Francis alive, young again and happy. He told Victor he bore him no ill will. It was, after all, an accident, a boyish prank gone horribly wrong, and that Victor should stop living with the guilt of it and enjoy the time he had left. He assured Victor that one day they would meet again, before shooting him dead with an arrow from his bow. The two boys squealed as they ran across the empty field, and a tear ran the length of the professor's cheek before nestling at the end of his nose. Travers laughed as the professor rubbed at the itch before returning to the halcyon sanctum of his dream.

In his office, Arthur dreamed of his parents, his mother laughing as her headscarf was almost blown off in the wind, his dad tanned and happy. They held hands as they walked along the Whitby front, sharing dreams, planning for their future. He sat on a bench and watched them as they passed, oblivious to his presence.

'I'm sorry I wasn't there for you Dad, at the end,' Arthur called out. His dad stopped and turned, a look of bemusement on his face.

'What is it, love?' asked Arthur's mother.

'Why, I could have sworn I...' Albert's sentence trailed off and suddenly his eyes met Arthur's and he smiled, lighting up his whole face.

'Arthur,' he said. Now it was his wife's turn to look puzzled.

'Arthur?' she said.

Albert McLaren placed his hand lightly on his wife's slightly swollen belly and sighed contentedly. 'The boy's name is Arthur.'

Dawn crept across the storm-tossed moor, the darkness retreating in its wake. It chased away the gloom and banished the angry rolling clouds far across the heath and out to sea. When it reached the station, it pressed against the glass, peering at the prone inhabitants before finding its way inside through gaps in the ill-fitting sashes. It embraced the sleeping passengers, its wispy tendrils like ghostly fingers tracing a path lightly upon their skin, chasing away the shadows and seeing them flee to the sanctuary of the corners.

Travers alone witnessed the coming of dawn, wearily and not without welcome. He walked across the room, his footsteps barely audible on the parquet, and flung open the waiting room door, stepping out onto the platform and breathing in the fresh, salty air. The sky was streaked with red, the occasional cloud hanging like shredded fabric, sheer, ethereal, weightless, the last clinging vestiges of the storm waiting to join their indefinable sisters across the water.

The station platform lay defeated about him, the tempest having done its worst, benches tossed aside, detritus blown onto the line, flowerpots smashed, and smaller trees uprooted. Signs were torn from their hoardings and lay to rest, mangled at his feet. He kicked aside a twisted advertisement for a local stockist of perambulators on Clarings Brook High Street and made his way towards the end of the platform and down onto the track, whistling as he went.

Travers felt peaceful at last. His work was done, his wings earned. In showing others the error of their ways, in hopefully setting them upon the right paths, he had atoned for his sin. The sin of taking a life, his own life. James C. Travers killed August fifth, nineteen-twenty-five when jumping into the path of an on-coming train from bridge three-sixty-one.

Travers walked awhile along the track, eventually disappearing into the fine mist at first light. Soon all that could be heard was a thin tuneless whistle, until that too was caught up on the gentle morning breeze and swept out to sea.

Lady Agnes Barnes, *née* Wallace, stepped out of the car and walked heavily across the drive and up the steps that led to the entrance of Beechings, the country house she shared, *had* shared, with her spouse, the eminent Sir Gregory Barnes KC. The corners of her mouth upturned slightly at the thought of her late husband.

Eminent indeed, Gregory.

She scoffed lightly at the thought. The weariness and the effects of the previous night's traumatic events seemed to have hit her all at once, and she leaned heavily on the arm of her housekeeper's husband for support. She knew the pain of Gregory's death and the grief at his loss were yet to come, because for all his faults, and there had been many, he was still her husband, the father of her son, and she had loved him once.

Her housekeeper, Mrs Allen, smiled kindly at the Lady Agnes, usually so well-coiffured but who suddenly looked so old and vulnerable. She took the lady's arm, leading her to the first-floor bedroom she had shared with her husband.

'I have warmed the sheets for you, Lady Agnes,' Mrs Allen said gently as she lowered the old lady onto the bed. Lady Agnes was asleep before her head hit the pillow.

'Goodnight Gregory,' she murmured before slipping into the safe confines of slumber's warm embrace.

Dorothy looked anxiously from the window of the little cottage she and husband Percy had shared these past seven years. She had paced the room for most of the night following a nightmare of her husband alone in a room full of evil spirits, wondering if tonight he would return home, if he was safe, where he would find shelter during the storm.

She was furious with him for causing her such worry, for his pig-headedness and for the blind jealousy that was threatening to end an otherwise happy marriage. The couple were childhood sweethearts and had married young. So what if she wanted a little time to herself, a hobby, something to broaden her horizons? It was only natural, wasn't it? She felt the anger flare up again, like a heat radiating from within. She turned to pace the room and caught sight of their wedding photograph on top of the mantle.

'Oh Percy,' she cried out loud, 'where are you?'

She was startled by a sudden noise outside, and she ran to the window to see a rather dishevelled, shame-faced Percy walking up the path. He barely had time to look up before his wife threw open the door and fell sobbing into his arms.

Professor Rose kicked at the shingle beneath his feet as his dog snouted amongst the seaweed washed up by the early morning tide. Overhead a curlew cried out, its lonely haunting call rending the still air and setting the professor's nerves on edge.

He sat awhile on a breaker and removed an envelope from his pocket. It was a letter from Lady Agnes, inviting him to pay her a visit in London. He fingered the edge of the paper until it became creased and tattered. He would write back to her at once, accepting her kind invitation, naturally he would. Or maybe he'd leave it, just for a day, or two.

He thought, as he often did, of the night he had spent in that lonely station waiting room on the storm-tossed moor. Of the people he'd been stranded with, of the secrets they had revealed, and he wondered at their lives going forward. Of the soldier and the charges he might face, of the stationmaster and Percy who were, as far as he knew, still working there. Of the young lady, Ellen, and her new job at the school, and, of course, of Lady Agnes and life without her husband of many years. And then he thought of the man, Travers, and how he had turned around everyone's lives, pushing them until their fraught nerves could stand no more, forcing their confessions, and of the epiphanies that invariably followed. Inducing them for the most part to make a clean breast of things, to seek forgiveness should it be needed, and to move on with their lives, unburdened... free.

Scout, his dog, barked at a crab that had run for cover beneath a large pebble. He pawed at the stone, but it was too embedded, too heavy to dislodge. He soon lost interest in the creature and began attacking a piece of driftwood, taking it between his paws and chewing on it as if it were a juicy bone.

The professor turned away and looked out to sea, letting his mind wander, thinking again of Travers and how, unbeknown to the man, he had followed him out onto the platform. Even after all the professor had witnessed that night, he had watched dumbfounded as the man, as the spirit of the man with whom he had spent the last few hours, had walked along the line and disappeared without a trace into the early morning mist.

As the professor slowly rose from his perch, his bones protesting with the effort, he suddenly felt a calmness, a feeling of well-being come over him. Turning to summon his dog, he began his steady walk home. As he walked, he fancied he could hear, as he had many times since the night at Little Hubery Station, the sound of a man whistling, distant and hollow above the gentle lapping of the waves.

Robert stood facing the board. The day he had been dreading had finally arrived. He gave his name, rank, and number to the panel, and with moist palms and a steely resolve, he began to relay his version of events. He told of how Powell had been spotted taking the child into the woods and was subsequently followed, but how they had quickly become lost in the thick of the trees. Of how the girl had been reported missing and her body found by villagers after a thorough search of the woodland. He told of how an inspection of the missing private's things had uncovered items, later identified by the parents of the village's children as belonging to them.

Robert reported how a group of angry fathers from the platoon and the village had spotted Powell and chased him, and how Powell had escaped to Haora on the back of a wagon. He told of how they had followed him to town and split into smaller groups, and how in losing his partner he had continued to search alone, and that was when he had witnessed the beating that led to Powell's death. He confessed to his shame in having done nothing to either prevent the attack or to help the victim afterwards. His words were heartfelt, and his head hung low as he confessed. He admitted it wasn't his intention to see justice served in that way and nothing on earth could have persuaded him to join in the lynching. He was moved to tears as he told of the men's anguish at witnessing the pain on the faces of the little girl's parents and of the horror they all felt in seeing the limp and lifeless body carried from the woods.

Robert realised he faced a dishonourable discharge from the army and potential imprisonment as an accomplice to the murder, but he felt it was his duty to report what he had witnessed. There could be no doubts in his mind as to Powell's involvement in the little girl's murder, nor that of his platoon mates' involvement in Powell's own, although he pointed out their exemplary records as serving officers of the British army, as well as being fine, upstanding citizens.

He'd had a strange experience while sat alone in the small office, waiting to face the board. A firm supportive hand had been placed upon his shoulder. He'd looked around quickly, but of course, there was no-one there. He had a momentary glimpse of the man, Travers, in his mind's eye. But instead of feeling angry and bitter towards one whose persistent goading had extracted his confession and forced his hand, he felt nothing but gratitude and warmth. Every bit as palpable as the relief Robert felt as he left the inquest. And afterwards, while waiting for his own wife and daughter, he sat again, quietly, his thoughts now only for the poor child and her parents.

An investigation into William Powell's past revealed him to be a very unsavoury character indeed, one with several run-ins with the law, although he had never been charged. It also told of his having no surviving relatives. The board brought a verdict of 'death by misadventure,' deciding to deal with the punishment of their men as they saw fit.

Robert was immediately stripped of his rank but continued for the time being to be stationed at Catterick Camp pending a court-martial. He was never again bothered by the shade of William Powell, as he had fulfilled his pledge and borne witness to the man's murder during the investigation. Besides, if what Robert believed was true, Powell faced a much harsher judgement himself, in the afterlife.

Ellen Potter looked up nervously at the ivy-clad buildings of the school that was to be her new home. She had made it, finally, and was to report to the headmistress, a Miss Naylor, on arrival. She stepped back on the gravel pathway, avoiding the well-kept lawns now over-shadowed by the ancient school buildings. It was quite dark now and the very tops of the chimneys were shrouded in mist.

She thought back to the night she and the others had been forced to spend in the waiting room at Little Hubery Station, of confessions made, of realisations reached, of epiphanies and fresh starts after the horrors they had been forced to endure. She hoped that they too had benefitted somehow from their strange encounter that evening.

Her thoughts turned to the newly-widowed Lady Agnes and her pledge to clear Michael Turner's name, the soldier Robert and his haunting admission. She wondered how he had faired during the investigation. And of course, the mysterious Travers, whom they had awoken to find missing. Travers with his amazing second sight and the ability to take each and every one of them to a point where they had to confess to their darkest secrets, and in doing so had faced their demons and were then able to go forward with their lives. Who could have guessed they all had such hidden skeletons? Quite the innocuous-looking group of strangers.

She suddenly felt as though she were being watched and looked to see a small, pale face observing her from an upstairs room Ellen presumed to be a dormitory. She smiled and waved to the little girl, who sank back into the shadows, undoubtedly afraid of a chiding for being up so late. An inexplicable shiver ran down Ellen's spine. Unbidden, Travers' words about atonement came to mind. They hadn't come across as sinister then, but there, standing alone in the dark, she felt a strange sense of foreboding and wondered at that moment what form her atonement would take.

From somewhere hidden amongst the ivy, she heard a door open, and a shaft of light lit up the gravel path, a welcoming beacon that caused Ellen to brush off any feelings of trepidation she may have had. It stretched out to the grass beyond before being swallowed by the darkness.

'Miss Potter? Is that you? Good heavens, such weather we've been having. Well come in, dear, come in...'

A thin, hawkish-looking woman in a stiff tweed skirt stepped out onto the pathway to shepherd the young teacher indoors. Ellen took one last glance up at the dormitory window, but the little girl had gone.

Arthur McLaren, stationmaster at Little Hubery since nineteen twenty-six, smiled on seeing the clock on his office wall, as the nine-fifty-five to Redcar left the station with not a second to spare.

'Regular as clockwork,' he said to no-one in particular as he rose to make a well-earned cup of tea. 'Drink, Colin?' he said to the young lad working the ticket office, Percy's replacement since he had been promoted and moved on to Waverley, a main line station up north. Colin nodded in thanks.

Arthur chuckled to himself as he watched two children, a girl and a boy, giggling while they played chase on the platform outside. He knew they were no more than shadows, waifs, a mere echo of what they once were, but he didn't mind. He saw them often since the night he met James Travers. Them and others.

He was looking forward to a wireless programme, the *Best of American Big Bands,* later that evening. Maybe he'd treat himself to a milk stout or two.

Still smiling, he gathered his papers from his desk, pigeon-holed a couple of letters, and stopping to collect his favourite mug from the mantelpiece, made his way through the booking office and into the kitchen.

Still smiling, he gathered his papers from his
desk, put on... a couple of letters, and stopping
to collect his favourite mug from the mantelpiece,
made his way through the book-lined. He and the
kitchen.

A Note from the Author

I hope you enjoyed Little Hubery and the few hours of escapism it afforded you. This first book of the Ellen Potter Mysteries encompasses all of life's little pleasures for me. A light-hearted book with which to curl up in front of a roaring fire on a cold winter's night, a traditional creepy ghost of a book, but never the stuff of nightmares. Railways, ghosts and the nineteen-thirties, all things dear to my heart.

Little Hubery is a work of pure fiction and for the purpose of enjoyment only. And it is here I apologise to railway experts, thirties buffs, and to our wonderful lads and lasses, veterans and those currently serving in the British army, for my crude lack of knowledge thereof. For although I did extensive research in these areas I am, I confess, no expert in any of them, so please be kind and don't pick holes! Rather enjoy Hubery for the work of fiction that it is.

Enough of my ramblings, for I'm sure you're all curled up and ready to sleep. Please, take Hubery and its message with you into dreamland, but be sure to leave the ghosts behind. Sweet dreams, dear reader and remember, there's nothing to fear. After all, none of this is real… or is it?

J.C. Phillips 2021

Coming Soon
From
Camelot Publishing Company

The
Ellen Potter
Mysteries
Book Two

Hush Now Child
By
J.C. Phillips

Ellen Potter is very much looking forward to her new life as head of English at St. Barnabas, an all-girls boarding school on the isolated Northumbrian coast. But when she stumbles upon the diary of a Victorian maid who lived and worked at the former Alderley Manor, a sinister tale of life in the once-stately home unfolds.

As Ellen find herself drawn deeper into the young maid's story, strange things begin to happen at the school, things reminiscent of Ellen's last encounter with the supernatural. Then one of her pupils confesses to witnessing terrifying paranormal events, and Ellen is convinced the schoolhouse is indeed haunted. Worse still, she comes to fear the child is in danger from malevolent spirits intent on doing her harm.

Should Ellen pursue her quest to find justice for the long-dead Victorian maid, or will she stir up echoes of things best left buried? Could awakening the dormant horrors within Alderley Manor bring grave danger to both Ellen and her pupil?

Hush Now Child, the second in the series of Ellen Potter Mysteries, is a terrifying supernatural tour-de-force that sees the awakening of Ellen's psychic powers and the beginning of her illustrious career as a psychic detective in 1930's Britain.

Read on for an excerpt from
Hush Now Child

The little girl awoke to muffled cries. She sat bolt upright and knelt on the bed, palms flat on the narrow window-ledge, and peered intently through the glass, but all she could see across the dark void were God's candles twinkling through the softly sighing upper branches of the old tree. Across the room, a gentle snore confirmed that her mother slept on undisturbed. She was about to settle down again when… there! The voices. Distant but somehow louder, as though raised in anger.

She crept from her cosy cot bed, the wooden floorboards rough beneath her bare feet. The child felt her way along the corridor and down towards the main staircase to the lower floors. She knew she would be in trouble if she was found wandering about the house in the dark, least of all on the main stair. As the daughter of a kitchen maid, she was expected to remain out of sight at all times, taking the spiral staircase at the rear of the house all the way below stairs only at times of work or to eat. She knew her place, but she was afraid of the cold, shadowy stairwell, and curiosity had gotten the better of her, that and an overwhelming feeling that something was terribly wrong.

As she crept down another flight, hugging the wall and keeping herself mostly in shadow, relishing the warmth and the feeling of carpet beneath her feet, so the sounds from the floor below continued. Once or twice her nerves almost got the better of her, and she had to keep herself from scuttling back up to bed like a frightened mouse. But the cries from below had taken on a distressed nature, as though someone needed help as a matter of urgency.

When she reached the next level, she followed the corridor round and came to a halt before her Ladyship's rooms. The door was ajar. She could see the flickering light of the fire dancing on the wall within. Could feel the draught from the open window curling around her feet. Without warning, a shadow filled the doorway and she jumped back behind a large oak tallboy, curling herself up as tightly as possible and squeezing into the corner between the wall and the cupboard.

'How could you?' her Ladyship cried. 'As if it's not bad enough, you keeping your whore within these walls, to now learn that *you* are the father of her bastard child.'

'Watch your language woman and keep your voice down,' the Master hissed at his wife. 'If anyone were to find out, there would be an outcry.'

'God forbid the family's good name be brought into ill repute,' his wife scoffed. 'God forbid anyone should learn that his Lordship, the master of the manor, is nothing but a cheat, a cad and a, a fornicator! I knew it! I should have trusted my instincts. Paid more heed to the whispers of the servants. I warned you, Charles. I warned you. Leave me. *Go!*'

The girl crept around from the side of the cupboard with the intention of sneaking back towards the stairs and out of danger, for she was certain if she were caught, the least she could hope for would be a severe thrashing. As she neared the foot of the stairs, she passed a long, low table. The clock upon it read three a.m. Long past her bedtime. Curiosity made her turn one last time to look. Her Master, poker in hand, had advanced towards his retreating wife. A sickening thud followed, and the woman was silenced for good.

Blood splattered the Master's coat and the fireplace and mirror behind him. The child bit down hard on her fist to prevent the scream that was even now rising in her throat and threatening to expose her. She turned back towards the stair, her whimpers barely audible, tears streaming down her cheeks.

But her muffled cry had not gone unheard, and the Master turned to see the shadowy form of his daughter scurry away up the staircase.

Ellen stepped from the car and took a hold of her small suitcase. It was a cold, damp, starless night, and when she walked through the grounds, she paused, listening as the caretaker's car pulled away. The old man had told her on the journey from the station (although he had said little else, so sullen was he) that he lived at the rear of the property, and unless she required him to drive her up to the door, he would drop her off at the gate and then drive around to his cottage. Ellen, not wanting to burden him any further, had assured him she would be fine carrying the luggage, but the second he left she felt inexplicably alone and lost and had thought of running after him.

'Pull yourself together, Ellen,' she chided, but shivered in spite of herself.

The moon cast an eerie glow over the wet slab stones, and the wind whispered through the distant trees, their skeletal branches blackened now against the milky, moonlit sky. Ahead loomed the old school building, and Ellen could see, in some of the windows, flickering firelight.

The hard standing had given way to well-kept, flood-lit lawns. A wide driveway separated two such lawns, and it was down this that Ellen now walked, assuming, and rightly so, that treading on the grass would be frowned upon. She stopped for a moment or two to inspect the impressive, ivy-clad building and was suddenly overcome by a feeling of being watched. As her eyes scaled the upper windows, she noticed a young girl, her face little more than a milky smudge, and as the woman got closer, she could just make out the child's large, solemn eyes. Ellen smiled and waved to the little girl, who sank back into the shadows, undoubtedly afraid of a scolding for being up so late.

She mounted a set of dimly-illuminated stone stairs, the two wall-hung coach lights partially obscured by ivy, and from somewhere hidden amongst the flora, double doors opened and a shaft of light brightened up the steps and part of the driveway beyond before being swallowed by the darkness.

'Miss Potter? Is that you? Good heavens, such weather we've been having. Well, come in, dear, come in…' A thin, hawkish-looking woman in a stiff tweed skirt stepped out onto the pathway to shepherd the young teacher indoors. Ellen took one last glance at the window above, but the girl had gone.

'Welcome to Alderley Manor and St. Barnabas School for Young Ladies. I am Grace Naylor, headmistress.'

The older woman offered a claw-like hand to Ellen, which Ellen took and was surprised by the firmness of the head teacher's grip. Miss Naylor's smile was genuine but held little warmth. She surveyed Ellen with a blatant directness that made the teacher colour, and she shifted uncomfortably from one foot to the other. Ellen herself was tall and slender, but Miss Naylor was the longest, thinnest woman Ellen had ever seen. Her neatly coiffured chestnut hair was peppered with grey and held in place by pins. Her features were sharp and pointed, and her colourless eyes were not exactly cold but guarded, giving away little of her thoughts and emotions.

'Thank you,' Ellen replied nervously. A quick look around found her to be in a magnificent but somewhat austere entrance hall with dark, heavy panelling and a vast oak staircase that separated into two mid-point, each flight heading off in opposite directions to a galleried landing framed by elaborate balustrades, and great, carved newels.

'So this was once a stately home? It's huge!' she gasped. 'How will I ever find my way around?'

'You'll get a feel for the place soon enough,' said Miss Naylor, not unkindly. 'Now, I believe you are the niece of our former head, Miss Francis? How is your aunt?'

At the mention of her aunt, Ellen saw a flicker of warmth in the other woman's eyes.

'I was her top pupil many years ago at St. Thomas of Aquinas in North Berwick,' Miss Naylor said with a smile, 'and she, my favourite teacher. She was the very first headmistress here at St. Barnabas, and I was assistant head.'

Ellen returned the smile. 'Yes, Aunt Iris spoke of you with some fondness. She has been unwell lately as you know, hence me beginning term a little late, but she is much improved now, I'm pleased to say.'

'Excellent, Miss Potter. Excellent.' The smile played about the head teacher's lips for a while, and she held the younger woman's gaze a little longer than Ellen was comfortable with.

'Kathleen,' said the head, abruptly turning, and Ellen saw a slim, pretty girl with fair hair emerge from a shadowy nook beside the staircase.

'This is Kathleen Stewart, our head prefect,' said Miss Naylor. The girl came forward shyly, and Ellen smiled warmly at her. 'Kathleen will show you to your room, Miss Potter, and you'll find a light supper has been left for you. I suggest you retire early, as you will be required to be up at six sharp to be prepped and to organise your lessons for later.'

Ellen, preparing to follow Kathleen, looked back at her head teacher.

'I bid you goodnight,' said Miss Naylor stiffly, any trace of warmth gone.

'Thank you,' said Ellen, 'and goodnight.' She allowed the child to lead her up the staircase, never once looking back at the headmistress but feeling the stony eyes on her until she was out of sight.

Ellen followed Kathleen up and along similar panelled hallways until the fourth floor, where the décor became plainer and the furnishing sparse. It was evident that at some point the house had been a grand home, and the staff accommodation was once the old servants' quarters. At the end of such a hallway, they came to a halt. Ellen thanked the girl for showing her to the door and passed gratefully inside. She was glad the introduction had been brief, for it had been a long day, and she found herself all of a sudden very tired.

Once inside, she was pleasantly surprised. The well-sized room, although simply furnished, was cosy and warm. A good fire blazed in the grate, and a large, comfortable-looking bed housed a faded eiderdown and some soft, fluffy pillows. There was a cupboard which locked and was large enough to house her clothes and her personal things and a desk with drawers at which she could prepare for her classes and do her marking. She thought she might even make a start on that romantic novel she'd been considering writing. She saw a good, strong bookshelf to house her personal collection, a sink for washing, and…

'Oh!' She almost squealed with delight on seeing an old wireless on the shelf.

Her attention was caught by a delicious smell, and she found herself drawn to a rapidly cooling bowl of broth and two great chunks of bread, which had been left for her on the desk. Finding herself suddenly very hungry, she tucked in with relish. Less than thirty minutes later saw her snuggled up beneath the eiderdown, sleepily watching the flames as the darkness closed in around her.

Ellen awoke unexpectedly and for a moment or two was confused by her unfamiliar surroundings. The fire had almost died out but for a few idling embers, which glowed like glittering jewels in the darkened grate. From somewhere close by an owl hooted. The moonlight poured in through the window, covering the floor with a silvery carpet, upon which danced the wind-tossed branches of a tree just beyond.

Around her the house was silent, nothing stirred, and Ellen wondered what it was that had awakened her so abruptly from such a deep sleep. She had been dreaming of the night she and six others had spent trapped by a freak storm in an isolated railway station. In the dream, she had stood apart from the others and was watching them from above as they huddled around the waiting-room fire. They seemed frozen in time. Only she could move about the room, effortlessly floating above them. Two elderly gentlemen appeared deep in conversation with a man in railway uniform. An elderly lady nursed a mug of something hot, for Ellen could see the steam rising from the cup. A soldier stood a little way from the others by the hearth, his cap resting on the mantle as he stared morosely into the flames.

She knew these people, but for some reason she could not remember their names. She had found herself, in her dream, floating into the chimney corner where a man sat alone in the shadows. All at once he looked up at her and she felt a moment's fear, and that's when she awoke from her sleep.

Ellen felt cold and hugged the eiderdown to her. The air moved around the room as though something had disturbed it, and dust motes danced in the pale moonlight. Suddenly, she froze and heard a sound that chilled the very blood in her veins. It was as if ghostly fingers were tapping at the window, asking to be let in. She thought of the wraith of Catherine Earnshaw in Wuthering Heights, and in her languid state, Ellen began to tremble. Outside, the noise continued, *tap, tap… tap, tap, tap,* lightly on the glass. Fear held her in its grip for what seemed an eternity. She felt as if she were still trapped in the midst of her dream, then all at once she knew she had to turn around and confront her tormentor.

Pushing the eiderdown to one side, she quickly sat up and swung around to face the window… and then she gasped, releasing her breath in a steady sigh of relief. She laughed and clutched at her chest before climbing back into bed and pulling the eiderdown up around her chin. Outside, tormented by the wind, the branches from the nearby tree tapped against the windowpane. Listening now fully awake, it was so obvious what the light tapping was. But that sound alone could not have been enough to wake her from her slumber, surely?

She was just dropping off again when she heard a child crying outside in the corridor and a faint scraping at the door. Fearing one of the girls was ill, Ellen ran to the door to see, but when she opened it, the noises stopped abruptly, and she found the corridor empty.

'Hello,' she called out, keeping her voice low so as not to wake her sleeping colleagues. 'Hello, is anyone there?'

A giggle from the end of the shadowy corridor told her there was, and she walked on down the hallway. The giggling stopped and she heard a sigh, right behind her left shoulder.

All at once, the passageway felt airless. She became lightheaded and had to hold on to the nearest doorframe for support. An icy hand gripped her heart. Then as suddenly as it began, the strange feeling disappeared, leaving Ellen dazed and bewildered in the darkened hall. Catching her breath, she quickly turned and made her way back to her room and jumped into bed. She pulled the eiderdown up to her chin and curled into a foetal ball.

Soon enough the wind abated, and the house fell into silence one more. Ellen took a while to sleep. When she did, her dreams were dark. The hours passed, but it seemed only minutes to Ellen when she again awoke, and even wrapped in her bedclothes, she suddenly felt very cold. Her legs felt like blocks of ice. She tried to move but found she couldn't. She tried to wriggle her toes, stretch her fingers… but was unable to. She felt helpless, vulnerable. Weighed down by something she couldn't see. It was as though an icy-cold hand clamped across her mouth, preventing her from screaming.

She struggled to breathe for the few seconds that seemed an eternity to one without air, and then she felt as though she were sinking, weightless and timeless through the void, deeper and deeper, warm, cushioned, surrounded by nothingness. She no longer felt breathless, for she no longer felt the need to breathe. She could hear voices, distant and hollow, as if muffled by time. A child's voice, a woman's scream. A man, angry, shouting! Somewhere amid the melee, she could hear her own name called over and over. Again, she tried to cry out. Again, she couldn't.

'Miss Potter, Miss…

The voice seemed closer than the others, shrill, like a ship's warning bell above a wishy-washy sea of distant voices.

'*Miss Potter*!'

An urgent knocking on the door and she jumped, finding herself wide awake and breathing hard, her heart thudding in her chest.

'Miss Potter. *Miss Potter*! You have overslept. You are to come quickly to the headmistress' office. You are way behind your time! Miss Potter?'